D0298348

THE SMALL HOURS

THE
SMALL HOURS

SUSIE BOYT

virago

VIRAGO

First published in Great Britain in 2012 by Virago Press

Copyright © Susie Boyt 2012

The moral right of the author has been asserted.

*All characters and events in this publication, other than those
clearly in the public domain, are fictitious and any resemblance
to real persons, living or dead, is purely coincidental.*

A CIP catalogue record for this book
is available from the British Library.

HB: ISBN 978-1-84408-825-6
C-format: ISBN 978-1-84408-913-0

Typeset in Garamond by M Rules
Printed and bound in Great Britain by
Clays Ltd, St Ives plc

Papers used by Virago are from well-managed forests
and other responsible sources.

MIX
Paper from
responsible sources
FSC® C104740

Virago Press
An imprint of
Little, Brown Book Group
100 Victoria Embankment
London EC4Y 0DY

An Hachette UK Company
www.hachette.co.uk

www.virago.co.uk

For Caroline Dawnay

18 Months Ago

She had glimpsed this ending a thousand times, lit it flatteringly in pinks and ambers, scripted its best lines, measuring the syllables and balancing out the soft rewarding looks. She would not, for all the world, have their final parting fraught. The last five minutes would be oceans of calm, dispassionate, blameless, textbook fashion. They would take their cues for conduct from the clock's prim tick.

She had woken early that morning in triumphant mood, the lovely dawn in bright white trousers, like a sailor, hoisting her spirits even further. It was unfailing and unarguable her transformation now and it was time to, if not spread her wings exactly, because obviously she was still – did it really need reiterating – a red-haired, earthbound woman of six foot one, serious-hearted, not given to literal flights of fancy, intense rather than intrepid and so on, but it was correct now *surely*, both parties agreed, for her, aged thirty-eight and a half, to walk quietly but with pride in the opposite direction, towards who-knew-what grand fate.

Please don't spoil things, Harriet self-instructed. You're nearly home. You've won. You are a fully functioning human survivor. You have, she reminded herself, the T-shirt. She had. She almost had. (There was a plain white butcher's apron emblazoned with *Forgive*

Everybody Everything in red flock italic script, blushing in spite of itself at the back of her underwear drawer.) She held this thought, twirling it about her person, flinging it up into the air like a ribbon-wrapped baton. She lowered her eyes and smiled ruefully at her loyal scuffed brogues. You are a fool, she murmured, but it was done with affection.

'I remember the first time I came here,' she began, for symmetry. 'Think I sat down in this chair and straight away said I wasn't feeling myself. That I never in my life quite had. How funny! It was as though at long last, after years of being put on hold, I was finally through to the complaints department.' She had been wry, at the beginning, in the face of loss, for about, oh, five seconds. To have your sadness tinged with pride and wit and a depth of understanding – that, after all, was suffering in style. 'I couldn't keep the humour up for long though, could I? But I'm glad I tried.'

Very quickly there had been nothing whatsoever to laugh about, and then, quite suddenly, she had shown herself intoxicated with despair. The disenchantment she had arrived with seven years ago was thorough, lead-weighted. The passing of morning to mid-morning and from mid-morning into early noon was a matter of high risk: there was no meaning, there was almost no self. It was a radical state for a human person – she knew she was out at the very edge of things, roaming, a stranger, whose landscape featured only wounds. But just look at me now!

Miss McGee inclined her head very slightly and softened her expression into a half-nod. They were about to close things down, it was agreed.

In four minutes Harriet would exit the room with all the elegance she could muster, dodging the Georgian breakfront bookcase for the very last time, skirting the demi-lune side table with walnut inlay and the bluntly faceted water carafe. She had an odd sensation borrowed from childhood; there must be strictly no opening up, no crashing into things in these last few seconds, for there would always be corridors with rows and rows of closed doors, but she had searched a great many of them and you could not make the flinging open of things your entire life's work.

The conversations that had gone on in this long, bow-fronted room! She had been taken, sketched, cosseted, allowed to unravel, challenged, stretched, re-educated. Miss McGee wasn't at all put out by the sad, unsanitary mess that had sometimes sat before her wailing with deranged ideas for further ritualised humiliations. The shifts came gradually and beautifully, the levers making infinitesimal movements and improvements, the gears caressed back into new alignments over years and years and years. The lines of inquiry broadened as the options changed. It was no longer a question of an avenging death or a liberating death. There was life to be lived! A certain amount of heavy industry resulted as you might expect: she was refitted with excellent hardware, was repointed and rehinged. They had grown for her, between them, two fresh parents, soft and green. It was daring stuff. The process was exhausting. Miss McGee resupplied her moorings, she revived and regaled her and finally – and the sweet pain of it was almost impossible to bear – this very afternoon would relinquish and unhand her, steadier, bolder and softer into the world. She had hoisted her sails and taught her where to find the wind and how to thread and knot the cable. It was expertly done.

She saw herself sometimes as a kind of dilapidated seaside pier, or faded tin horses on an old carousel, still hurtling round, with a bit of grace, modest and clanking yes, but with blues and pinks and bits of gold remaining and charm and other things to admire about them: tenacity, courage, cheer.

There were three minutes remaining now, two minutes fifty-five outstanding of this seven-year, three-times-a-week, what-was-it-exactly? For it wasn't a sentence or a phase or an innings and although it wasn't the opposite of a love story, it could hardly be styled a romance. Opposite, Miss McGee sat calmly and with unique dignity, fingers laced loosely in the folds of her skirt. Two minutes twelve.

To know someone well without a scrap of evidence. Was there a hero bold who held Miss McGee's heart? What, for that matter, was her daily lunch routine? Of course, it was probably vegetable soup, of a refined calibre, naturally, half a sandwich to follow, on some exquisite bread, but it wasn't quite the same as actually knowing.

Of course, Miss McGee didn't for a second give anything away. Her garments, well fashioned from high-class materials in plain shades, were almost extravagantly nondescript: skirts, jerseys, neat shift-style day dresses, shoes, nothing creased or mended or outlandish, yet what they said, these assorted, irreproachable clothes, depended on the way they were worn, and the way they were worn was exactly what it was impossible to read. There was nothing in her you could pin down, her hair of uncertain colour, her skin of indeterminate years. She was a sort of mouse *de luxe*; in fact she was Supermouse. She could be anything you wanted.

'It's nearly time, isn't it?' Harriet said. The clock's black hands on the table between them could not tell a lie. 'Nearly time,' echoed Miss McGee, with an indulgent quarter-smile.

And then Harriet could not wait a moment longer, her walls came down, her banks broke. 'You, you've just helped me so much,' she cried out to the woman opposite her who had loved her more than anyone she knew. 'I wouldn't be here if it weren't for you. Wouldn't want to be. Thank you! Thank you so so much! I thought endlessly about a present, the perfect thing, but nothing seemed good enough – good enough! – and then, I suppose, what I'm certain I knew you'd most like from me was nothing at all, and so I reined myself in. Which doesn't exactly come naturally, as you know. I do wish I'd brought something now. For my own sake in a way. When I act against my feelings I always get into hot water.' She spoke the simple words as though a motto she had memorised.

Harriet closed her eyes briefly. Miss McGee had torn away great swathes of unfactual landscape: they had done it together. The colour of everything was compromised when the world failed you at every turn. Miss McGee saw this completely and she saw just as strongly that it wasn't at all true. They resituated things, they resuscitated and reframed. They had a rampage. Both admitted after time that their subject had a lot of potential. This child they were raising together could be powerful and headstrong – some of its judgements were entirely tyrannical – but these could be good things.

'And I saw such a beautiful bowl from the nineteen fifties, quite severe, architectural somehow, very dark brown with a thin white line beneath the lip. It was so discreet. And I very nearly got it for you. I would have done, but there was a tiny chip at the base I wasn't happy about, thought it might tempt fate somehow. Not even sure what I mean by that. Send me scurrying back before the year was out perhaps. Wish I had got it now, perhaps it's not too late, but – anyway, for now, a million thank yous!'

Miss McGee moved her head a fraction. Was there a twelve-degree upsurge in her thinnish, shallow smile? Was she about to utter '*De rien!*' or 'The pleasure, my good fellow, was all mine'? Or 'Oh! Come *come*, my dear.' Miss McGee, intelligent, Kleinian, remote, had never once called her my dear. It would have been to them both utterly scandalous.

Harriet had not quite stopped talking. One minute twenty-two, she saw. 'It's odd in a way but for years and years, when you think about it, I put my happiness completely in your hands, didn't I? And for some of those years, probably for most of them, you were the most important person in my life and I suppose, you know, what I'm trying to say, I think, is that's a very big thing to lie between two people.'

Miss McGee nodded. 'Yes it is,' she said.

'And I suppose, I can't help thinking was it very, I don't know, very mad of me almost to throw myself into things so, so fully, to give myself over to it so completely, the process? I mean I'm sure not everyone does that . . . Of course, obviously it may have helped things to work, helped the things we were talking about to . . . to take, but I don't know . . .'

Miss McGee looked at her with a sort of shimmering frankness. 'It was brave of you,' she said. 'It was very brave.'

Tears started in the suburbs of Harriet's eyes. She spoke slowly and with emphasis. 'Well, you say brave, but really it was you . . . what I mean is, it was you who made throwing myself into things seem like the wisest and the safest, seem like the only thing to do.'

There. There was their perfect ending gleaming lustrous before them. Both women exhaled. Harriet blinked. All it would take now was for her to rise from her chair and murmur another thank you and issue a firm goodbye, then walk clearly and with strong direction out of this room once and for all. But, it transpired, there was a postscript. She was still sitting firmly in her seat. She had always

been hopeless at secrets. Well, that was not strictly true, but—
Besides, could you really, sensibly, squander your last thirty-seven
seconds with the best person you knew?

'You know, I just keep thinking what I really want, what would
really help me now would be to do something . . . I keep saying to
myself, at least I think it's to myself, Why can't I do something a bit
grand, I'd love that, you know, something a little bit amazing, just
this once? Put what I believe into practice, because I've kept my
head down for so long. I've had to and I do understand why, and
there was a time when there wasn't a choice or anything, but maybe
I won't have to be quite so cautious in the future. So modest about
everything.'

Did Miss McGee's glance widen? Was there a hint of swallowed
alarm or was it merely indigestion, a mal-mauled morsel making its
mark?

'Grand in what way?'

Harriet saw she was about to let the beast out of the bag, it was
clawing and scratching at the thin skin at her wrists, but she would
at least aim for a casual tone.

'Did I say that I've found the perfect building? For the school,
I mean.'

Miss McGee would match her ounce for ounce in nonchalance,
of course.

'You've not mentioned anything about a building, or about a
school.'

'I'm going there straight after this. I'm meeting the estate agent
for the third time. He's maddening! Anyway, the money's coming
through from the will next week, the lawyer says, so the timing
couldn't be better. It means so much to me that he wanted me to
have this money, that he trusted me with so much. Because if you

dislike someone or you think your daughter's nuts or crackers you don't heap a pile of money on her head, do you? That really *would* be mad. And despite everything, he was always careful to me.'

Miss McGee sat there, thoughtful, but not commenting. Harriet, undiscouraged, looked away. 'It's in Winchester Crescent, I don't know if you know.' She gestured in the general direction. 'I'm going to call it Winchester House, I think. It sounds a bit severe, I suppose, but it's dignified. I couldn't stomach Little Acorns, or Sweet Beginnings or Teensy Toes or whatever these places are called. They sound so sinister, like schools in a newsflash after everyone's been shot down ...'

'Ah,' said Miss McGee.

'Anyway, my idea is our standards will be sky-high. I don't mean striving for academic excellence which when applied to three and four year olds is nonsense anyway. I just mean we'll be excellent about everyone having a really wonderful time. I want to make a sort of paradise for the children. There's a beautiful garden, full of junk at the moment, old sinks and everything, but there's a huge willow tree and loads of blackberry bushes and wild flowers. I don't know. I suppose because my family don't like me I always think I should keep my head down in life but the truth is I'm really good with children. I know I often grate on people and I always have to hold myself in but children accept me for some reason. Don't have to make myself smaller, saner, stupider ... Since I've been volunteering at the hospital I've realised that ... I mean they *love* me in the children's ward. They beg me not to leave when I go home.' It was foolish to speak in such a way, talking oneself up in the American style, and there were streaks of embarrassment ripening on her neck and cheeks, but it felt important to try to— 'I think I'm going to make the school almost *too* lovely.' Soppy and flabby

8

in her mouth and inadequate, the word sent a grin to her lips none the less.

She was already proud of what she would achieve. 'The main playing room will be on the first floor, it's L-shaped with two fire-places and floor-to-ceiling windows, it's in a really rough state now but it's easy to see how, I mean, I suppose . . . ' She cleared her throat formally. 'And so, what I want to say while I still have the chance is, and I'm not sure why it matters quite as much as it does, and it's not as though I want or need your blessing exactly or your endorse-ment or approval, but I suppose, I mean, what I'm wondering, and I don't know why I've waited until the end of our very last session after seven years – seven years! – to bring it up but what do you think about it? About my plan? About my idea of opening a nurs-ery school with the express purpose of giving the children who come to me a really really joyful and idyllic start that will set them up for life?'

Miss McGee stirred very slightly in her air-blue wing chair, gazing at her patient not warmly exactly, not coolly, not without friendship but not with passion either, for those pale eyes were naturally glassy pools and awfully hard to decipher and, although her bearing was kindly in the abstract, you never knew how per-sonal anything was allowed to be. She unlaced very very gradually her fingers and took her hands from her lap to her sides. And then she said the only two words she *could* say. She said, 'It's time.'

With the final session unequivocally over, on the spotless shal-low steps of Vincent Court, Miss McGee's handsome red-brick mansion block, Harriet lingered taking deep breaths, half wanting to lie down proudly like an expanse of marble floor, but 'Come on!' she chided as though addressing a recalcitrant child. As she stepped through Miss McGee's immaculate neighbourhood, the thin rain beat a tiny pressure on Harriet's scalp. She sagged slightly, well anyone would, but there was work to be done. She mustn't grow stagnant, with birds and brambles and even squirrels settling in her skirts! She attempted to stride purposefully and with great attention as she was clumsy and knew herself to be and minded. There was a violet dinginess to the dusk now, the city drizzle faintly sordid. A cake shop went by with lacy white iron street chairs and tables under a scalloped grey awning and inside a woman in a slit skirt and polished hair was stabbing a coffee éclair with a spoon. Dirty drops from the awning fell on Harriet's red cheeks. She would never be a slit-skirt person, she thought.

The sky darkened and the rain thickened and thickened again, the rough wind on her face like the knot of a coarse woollen scarf. Harriet – coatless – saw the heroic orange light of a taxi and flagged it down. The driver sighed sharply when she said the name of the street, as if it were the last place in the universe he wanted to go, but it's just his unfortunate manner, she thought, she had one herself she'd been told. In the confines of the taxi things were safe and warm. A small television started up suddenly, blasting an antique comedy show with machine-gun laughter. She switched off the volume but the picture held: a bedsit and two men and two pints of beer and a winded brown sofa and a parakeet. A tree-shaped, pine-scented air freshener hanging by the driver's mirror assaulted her sinuses through the glass divide. She sniffed and her eyes grew watery.

Longing – a syrupy ache – for Miss McGee spread about her. She shook her head; had they made their ending too soon? Miss McGee was a sort of perfection. The sum of her, it was no exaggeration, contained everything a person could possibly need. She was like a human department store; one that stocked only items of the utmost quality, yet the prices were awfully keen. It was all there, neatly contained for the merest passing glance: fierce discretion, acute judgement, intelligent warmth, unconditional regard. On the top floor ('Going up!') weren't there the most dazzling brain cells stacked in orderly, well-lit display?

'And now you're *gone!*' Harriet filled the hollow taxi with the word, throwing her hands into the air with great mock woe. 'I am Miss Havisham on wheels,' she murmured, 'sans cake.' She was smiling.

'What's that, miss?' The driver turned his head.

'Oh, just more of my nonsense,' she said bashfully. She could bid the driver to stop and retrace their steps right away. 'It's your boomerang child!' she would cry. She shook her head. Ridiculous to pretend you have been ripped from the breast. They had spent the best part of a year in the winding down, after all. Yet if only Miss McGee had extravagantly ventured 'My door's always open' or 'Don't be a stranger, dear' or, waving, 'Do keep in touch' at the last. She couldn't possibly have made such a statement, Harriet did see, but she might have done so all the same.

At odd moments, late at night or in the spiteful small hours of the morning, Harriet wrote the chapters of self-help books in her head. Not *Live Your Best Life*, not *Open the Gateway to Plenty*. No, her fragile guides had modest names like *Staying Reasonably Cheerful* and *Putting Up with Stuff*. For *Putting Up with Stuff*, a wistful treatise on how it's fine sometimes to sigh and shrug and decide not to kick up a stink every *single* time, she liked devising visualisation techniques. Imagine you are face to face with someone only mildly annoying. Imagine looking that person straight in the eye and saying firmly and clearly, 'Oh all right then. Never mind.'

Trouble was, it was always you who were annoying.

'All right then. Never mind,' she said to herself out loud.

As they turned into Winchester Crescent she paid the driver and ran up the steps where the chubby estate agent was waiting impatiently though she wasn't quite a minute late. It was almost dark now and his forehead was saffron yellow from the streetlight. UNDER OFFER proclaimed the sign in thick red capitals, and she flinched for a second, before remembering this boast of possession was her own badge of success. Had she ever wielded such power?

'We'll start at the top this time, shall we? Or the *bottom?*' There was half a snigger in his tone as he pronounced the word. He didn't know what to do with her, that was it, she was six inches taller than he was, her shock of long red hair a challenge to his embarrassed pate, near-bald at what was it, thirty-three? He shunted open the door muttering, 'After you.' His phone rang continually and he barked 'Martin Brooks' into the handset. 'Elaine Elaine Elaine,' he said, 'what part of no do you not understand?'

Harriet glided past him – past his long pointy shoes that were buffed to a high shine – through the broad hall, up the stone staircase to the top and down again, darting fondly in and out of every room.

For once, there was no dilemma. It was a house built for great emotional scenes. The three long windows on the first floor, the bright dry attic with its views of several thousand roofs, the broad original cupboards that lined the basement's walls, large enough for childish espionage. Harriet paused in the hallway, peeling back the front door and sitting down on the doorstep. She flattened the creases of her skirt, stretching out her tall legs, her feet and toes, until both her shoes clopped off. The street being half bad did not much trouble her: bald and sour-smelling; cracked stucco; six or nine bedsits to some of the houses, but the surrounding roads were verging on the grand. From a high window at the next door place a woman beat a carpet roughly, sending down a thin rain of dust and crumbs. At the corner where the pub was an elderly man sat extended on the pavement, his plum-coloured toes visible through ruptured tennis shoes. He chipped away at the crusted skin on his forearm with a small paring knife, but it did not matter. She had chatted to him on her last visit. He said he was from Oughterard, which was mentioned in *The Dead*. He drank steadily from a bottle of fortified wine. She imagined him issuing valiant similes with respect to fine mornings and even finer ladies at large in them. The off-licence opposite the pub was named in rainbow iridescent letters Drinkers Paradise.

Back inside, to the agent's additional exasperation, she made one more breathless sally to the top, a spry metal ball on a vertical pin table perhaps. It was almost more excitement than she could bear. The stairs were solid under her, supportive, almost matronly. The roof looked sound and was of largely new blue-black slate tile. On the way down she counted the five fine marble fireplaces – one with cherubs – examining the elaborate cornicing to all the principal rooms. Underneath the perishing red lino on the first floor she spied glimpses of golden parquet. You had to look a layer below what you could easily see. Cookers and basins lurked in most corners, lavatory pipes and wires and pulled sockets and grazed black sacks full of failed items were piled up in the passageways, and dirt clung to everything so thoroughly that it seemed like a sort of deranged indoor weather, but Harriet had never been afraid of hard work. The price, though impressively high, was not impossible. It was widely accepted things had slumped. Everything hung on the planning permission now. You had to act quickly.

The amount she had been left was a large one. It needed rising to for it was a third of the sum of her father's working life. You couldn't just spend without real intent, turning blind eyes to shocking prices, start being profligate with the radiators and the greengrocer's bills. It was a great compliment to her, she felt it keenly; a figure that required ambitions, projects, inspiration. There was an equation that needed to be balanced. It had been, for one thing, so thoroughly earned.

That her father's heroism had been confined to his place of employment was something she had decided years ago. His entire posture was different when you saw him at work. He had loved the bank – he oversaw its insurance operation which he had helped to establish – and he had given himself up to it completely. In his dark suiting and snow-white shirting, sitting in an important chair, clutching a rolled gold fountain pen and weighing carefully his words, he was very nearly immaculate. The bright elm plateau of his desk brought something lively to his gaze, caused spots of dry glitter in his eyes. He had, in the bank's own exacting terminology, *lived the job*. That was all – it wasn't personal. There had never been, as far as she knew, anyone else. And besides, they had had their moments. She could not have borne the daily humiliation of no good memories. He had taken, for example, a very keen interest in her schooling. The establishments she had attended catered to the intelligent highly-strung. Some of the pupils had been so self-conscious that they sat on their little chairs as though perched on precarious cliffs.

She had been hurt at the burial by the depth they let him into the ground. She hadn't known they put people in so deep. It was like a well. She felt her father crying out to her as he went down roughly into the soil, the narrow gleaming coffin jerking, dangerous, lower and lower, the handles clattering in the dead afternoon. It was an outrage what was done. She sent a hand up into the air and shook it wildly in silent appeal to her mother, to her brother – DO SOMETHING – but their faces and their bodies were tightly closed against her. He needed to be higher up, nearer to the grass, closer to the light.

'Done, are we nearly?' the agent bellowed up the stairwell.

She gazed out through a tall rear window. Soon the fruit would ripen in the garden. She saw a cluster of girls, mini-heroines all, transporting berries in the lifted skirts of their checked pinafores, lips stained purple and flecked with seeds. She mapped it out in her mind, allowing the full delirious span of it, the pear trees, the raspberry canes, deciding exactly where they would grow the cress, the lettuces and parsley, carrots and potatoes, for the school lunches. She saw cranes and cormorants and the bright chipped paintwork of a gypsy wagonette. The wallpaper in the children's boot-room – crisp salady ferns on a background of the mintiest blue. If she could come to some sort of arrangement with the neighbour, it might be possible to keep a Shetland pony, strawberry roan. She stroked, in her head, its speckled flanks. Chickens at the very least. She saw the fingers of four small hands galloping up the keys of a grand piano, in what would be the music room. She dreamed of the same duet receiving great ovations around the capital cities of the world.

She stopped briefly to accuse herself of over-acting, but why couldn't a school aim high?

On the second floor, in its tender new studio incarnation, a cluster of girls would gather at their easels, making clear bold brush strokes on white cartridge paper: autumn flowers and fruit arranged on swathes of silk or devoré, a glistening sea bass; why not a life model now and then?

One street away there thrived a bustling fruit and vegetable market whose operators might be bribed to include small helping girls. She grinned at the thought of baby costermongerettes. Could the Italian café at the corner prove a promising playground for miniature waiting staff?

'Make the ideal family home with a bit of work,' the agent muttered, pinstriped, presumptuous, banal. 'D'you have a big family?'

'Soon,' she said. 'I'll have one soon.'

When Harriet's school was closing down, two years later, when the eighteen rush-matted stools were carted out to the local dusty auction rooms where they would be sold as a job lot with six pink Formica tables and a blue clapboard doll's house with wraparound porch, by the half-derelict, red-nosed auctioneer who couldn't help cursing at the thought he was in a room half filled with children's toys and even worse than that children, and worse still, little girls actually bidding, schoolgirls who had all the disadvantages of their sex with none of the fringe benefits ... Harriet, sitting on the school's front step, chin propped thoughtfully on the briny curve of her knuckle, wondered if she might have played things differently, both practically and mentally, and she decided, on the contrary, that her school was by far the best thing she had ever done.

First Day

Harriet Mansfield stood behind the front door taking deep breaths, transferring her weight from one leg to the other, like an athlete in preparation. It was nine seventeen. Children and parents were gathering in the street outside, she could see them through the spy-hole, a knot of highly groomed mothers, lithe and flinty-hearted, their voices drifting in through the open ground-floor windows as they tried to communicate care.

A woman in maroon leather breeches and pale towering evening sandals bent to sniff the wild expanse of vivid lavender which Harriet had sown in lead planters at the entrance, to promote calm.

A woman in a tangerine fringed scarf seized a purple stalk or two. She shredded the powdery flowers in her palms. Harriet steeled herself against such casual violence.

Concentrate, Harriet thought, she was winning and she would win. She felt ecstatic suddenly, determination and happiness bursting on her cheeks and lips. She had allowed herself to wear her handsomest dress of red crêpe and over this had added, as a sensible precaution, a brand-new chef's half-apron, the thick white weave punctuated by minuscule black pin-pricks. She was Red Riding Hood! She was Coca-Cola! The overall effect of her, she gathered it to her heart, might even be Santa. It was not a day for self-censure. The glow of success was ripening in blotches on the skin of her arms, her tall frame elongated further by unarguable pleasure. So springy and optimistic was her outlook it was really as though all her joints and limbs had been refashioned from new elastic.

'This is my very first day at nursery,' Alice was announcing to the lens of her father's video camera.

Harriet had taken on a sort of half-slum, the walls veined with mould, the corners smoking with rat shit, and through tenacity (and insight and instinct) she had created something quite exceptional. The purple lavender, lush and buoyant, sent its powerful scent out into the street. The path to the front door was tiled with brilliant black and white. She had hired a team of four staff, Honey, Tina, Serena and Linda, inspired allies all – well, Linda was a little stolid but her competence with admin and marketing could not be denied. A school of one's own, it was more, much more, than a home. It was the most romantic moment of her life. She tried out the thought, unsure if it were wholly true, but the idea appealed.

So she had possessed the money with which to do the job, well, with that came no guarantees. Their old family accountant, Mr Fletcher, grave and cautious at their meetings, trying to enter into the idea of it, almost gave himself a seizure. It was late afternoon, the last time, and it was warm and he murmured that as he had known her all her life might he be forgiven for removing his jacket?

'Absolutely.'

Underneath he was held together by green jacquard braces. He cleared his throat. There was something cracked about her scheme he needed to view as intact, she thought. '*So*, and do correct me if I'm wrong, let me get this clear, you are firmly *not* hoping to make money from this enterprise. Rather, you plan to let the money from your father's estate subsidise this project. You expect, as it were, to make losses, certainly for the first three years. And any profit that should occur you will use to fund free places for local girls of slender means?'

Harriet nodded. The fellow dabbed his brow with a flash of yellow paisley but he did not tell her she was wrong.

Through the spy-hole Harriet watched little Lucy gnawing at a fluted golden brioche.

As they were not around to celebrate her Harriet tried to bring a parent's pride to the proceedings. In her mind, over time (with the help of Miss McGee) she had reconstituted an approachable older man and a chestnut-haired softish woman who really liked her. 'Your instincts are GOOD,' they would say to her, 'and your understanding. Trust yourself. Be bold.'

It was not that she needed great skeins of bunting and brass fanfares at every turn exactly, it was more . . . Look at what you have achieved, she remarked jaggedly into the gleaming hall. She dealt an impetuous glance of triumph at the schoolmistress who had remarked, twenty-five years earlier, that she was of difficult character. She remembered a boyfriend when she was twenty who compared her to a bread knife, a serrated one, which made her laugh then cry.

Her head, naturally, teemed with slights and disappointments. Allies and foes, allies and foes. It was just the weather, but she did wish it were otherwise.

Her mood largely cooled now, Harriet reprimanded herself severely. What is wrong with you? she hissed. Why must you always always always bring a cracked skull to the feast? But there were still a few minutes remaining for a spot of first aid. You're just sad because you've done this on your own, but that's also a happy thing. It's completely your creation, your idea, your life. Really, it's your dream come true you're living. Many people never do. She smoothed down her apron's immaculate dry lustre. She brought to mind Miss McGee's well-modulated nods and smiles, her routine darting ironic glances, her intelligent half-laughs, her loyalty, her cautious, highly specific semi-reprimands. 'You were very brave', she strained to hear the woman say.

At last she felt the fire returning to her body, a burning sensation on her cheek and a ring of colour at her lips; perhaps it was not quite as strong as before, but that wasn't necessarily a bad thing. She needn't blaze and crackle like a fairground. It didn't have to be as strong as that.

She glanced behind her where her staff stood in bright chaotic clothing, a little eager chorus line, with fifteen years' experience between them: Honey, a soft artistic honey blonde; Linda the administrator, brisk and mature; Tina, a dynamic former dancer; and Serena, whose erect and bustling presence made you think of blue and gold first-prize rosettes. Their broad grins and hopeful, jittery limbs told her they were as fully braced for a morning crammed with delights as she. Here goes! She bestowed extravagant smiles upon these tremulous four who, easy-going as they all were, would rather be eaten by sharks than misplace one single apostrophe. 'Five four three two one,' she said, then she muttered a minuscule Latin prayer, cleared her throat, bit her lip, released it, drew back the latch and opened the door to greet the families who looked up at her from the pavement with large imploring eyes.

Just then an ancient-looking painted market cart went by, dressed with pyramids of green and violet artichokes nestled in squares of blue tissue, ushered by a man in a cap and pale, rolled shirtsleeves. He looked as though he might have wandered over casually from a nearby film set. He looked as though he might, at a push, burst into song.

Then parents and children began traipsing up the front steps and unwrapping themselves in the great front hall. Harriet greeted every child by name. Soon you could hear the sounds of children exclaiming at the activities that had been set out for them in the large first-floor drawing room above: the hospital corner with real crêpe bandages; the vast train track in a figure of eight; the night nursery with twelve enamel beds for dolls and animals; the polka-dot flamenco dresses suspended from gingham hangers on a bright chrome rail. Harriet ascended the staircase, scooping up the two last children and balancing them on her hips like a majestic Grecian urn.

Upstairs the parents, who had been pressed to stay for as long as the children wished, stood in clusters, casting their eyes about the triumphant room: the walls painted in the clearest pink, the pale parquet gleaming, the rose-coloured linen play house, the play café where on small round tables lay menus and bud vases and small waiters' pads: *sweets, sundries, fish, roll and butter, grills, roasts, hot beverages.*

The second floor was for painting and crafts and general mess making, with three carpentry benches; the ground floor for gymnastics, music and dance. Out of view on the very uppermost attic floor with views of ten thousand roofs or more, a rainbow of grey from dove to Quink, were Harriet's simple quarters: her desk and chair and bed in one large room with sloping walls, cupboard doors hiding or revealing the strip of crimson kitchenette, her bathroom with its washer-dryer and wardrobes and her father's blameless red velvet George III chair.

Harriet's heart swelled sharply with love and its severe reverse emotions. She brimmed with all she had and all she lacked. Wiping her eyes, she composed herself once more and not unkindly. *Bearing Up* was a book she could write in her sleep. She tried to be witty about it, casual, debonair. It was a basic fact of human life, everyone said so, that family was never remotely impressed by anything you did.

In the story corner, Honey's kind, clear, young, blonde voice was mesmerising. '*Once upon a time there were two little dogs called Eggs and Bacon. Eggs had a yellow collar and a white lead and Bacon had a red collar and a pink lead. And Eggs had a yellow and white striped sleeveless fluffy woollen knitted jacket and Bacon had a red and pink striped sleeveless fluffy woollen knitted jacket. And they lived in a tall white house next to a large green park with their owner Amelia who was three years old and she had a blue and white striped seersucker coat and black shiny lace-up shoes.*'

A young mother approached Harriet, narrow and elegant in double-breasted herringbone tweed. Her large soft mouth was trembling, her movements approximate, slightly unreal like a high building viewed through fumes. 'It's just all so lovely,' she said. 'I'd like to stay here for ever. It's about the loveliest thing I've ever seen. It's like a heaven for children. It's almost too much. You've made everything so beautiful. I'm afraid I'm going to cry.' She collapsed into watery giggles, and had to be sat down and found a drink.

Later, Harriet spread out at the sky-blue craft table and started to make a Tudor family from old lace and scraps of withered blouse. Evie and Lily and Mia were attempting the lady's seven children in descending sizes. On the table a book was wedged open at a Picasso collage. Some Schubert songs were playing quietly. In the basement kitchen Honey was vigorously juicing oranges while macaroni softened in a cauldron on the stove. In the next door office Linda was cropping some photos on the computer for the new prospectus. On the ground floor Tina was attempting to take a tap class: 'Brush brush shuffle,' she sang out as Mr Gelbard, an ancient pianist bribed from the local community centre, played 'Gotta Get My Old Tuxedo Pressed' with almost too much emotion. In the garden, with three girls to help her, Serena was planting spring bulbs. 'Hey! Don't eat the worms, guys,' Harriet heard her call. On the first floor some of the more anxious mothers were whispering together by the window seat. To the rear four girls playing hospitals wrapped each other's limbs in bandages, wailing at their recherché ailments. 'My poor head feels like a sugary bun,' cock-a-hoop with mirth.

Harriet blinked and bit her lip. Was it provocative, her permanent Cornish pasty grin? If happiness stems from difficulties overcome, she mused, dislodging some stringy gobs of glue from her cuff and smearing them on to the pocket of her apron, then she was certainly— But on the other side of the room there was sudden live commotion. Flora, the small sensitive girl with the nut-brown hair, was sobbing noiselessly, flinging herself repeatedly into the skirts of her mother's bone-coloured coat. Harriet moved over to them at speed.

'I have to go, darling,' the woman said calmly and firmly, repeatedly, professionally, as though obeying instructions in a care manual she had read. 'Mummy would *love* to stay but she *has* to go.' Mean things delivered in a soft voice always put one in mind of sadism. Unpeeling her child's arms from her knees, with dexterity, only to see them latch immediately again on to her hem, unlacing her daughter's fingers from the fabric, giving her a slight shove, and taking a fast sidestep, the mother's slender body nimbly evaded the small girl's clutches. There were wails, there was a beating of fists and utter incomprehension from the child. 'The sooner I go, the sooner I can come back, darling. You'll have a lovely day. Mummy has to go,' she said from the other side of the room and with that she perfected her vanishing act, exiting the threshold, gliding not inelegantly down the stairs and through the front door whose latch clicked fiercely shut against the vivid screams of her daughter who was crashing over the stairs now, calling after her bitterly, stunned and ashamed at her beautiful relation who had done what mothers aren't quite meant to do. Now the child lay pink and watery in a little tragic heap on the coir matting in the hall at the mouth of the door.

Harriet regarded the child with excessive warmth, knelt to meet her, sat down crossed-legged on the floor. Flora climbed aboard her headmistress, lolling her head on to Harriet's shoulders, feeding an arm round Harriet's broad back.

'She's gone to see my auntie in hospital,' Flora said. 'She's always going.'

'Oh, I'm sorry,' Harriet said. 'I'm really sorry about that.'

Flora gazed up at her headmistress with such a heavy weight of feeling that Harriet flushed.

She stroked Flora's head and sang her the lilting chorus of her favourite song. 'Hi-Lili, Hi-Lili, Hi Lo, Hi Lo, Hi-Lili, Hi-Lili, Hi Lo.' And the strangest thing, although the force and concentration of the child's hurt and rage were impressive and extravagant – and this was quite delightful – she could hardly have been easier to console. It was the best kind of personality to have, without question, to feel things very deeply but to allow yourself to take comfort readily and with equal gusto.

Harriet's pride surged, rose-coloured, measureless. Nothing could warp or diminish her now. It was as though – yes – even to ease the dead from their coffins and stand them on their feet might lie within her – *Do Come Off It!* by Harriet Mansfield. She smoothed down her spattered white apron firmly, so giddy with pleasure that she wished there were a mirror near or even a dashing young photographer, or – although this was far-fetched – a courtly portraitist with canvas and brush and a chevalier's extravagant moustache, to record the fact.

In the Space of Three Minutes

On Thursday Harriet took the older girls on a little tour of the neighbourhood, scrapbooks fluttering at their sides. The market glowed and hummed: there was bustling at the fruit stall, a jostling queue, impatient complaints, near-indecipherable fast patter. 'He's saying "One pound a scoop, any scoop for a pound",' Isabella clarified. 'At the farmers' market in the country, some of the mens say it, I think.' She was so intelligent, almost scholarly, in her measured observations.

'You're right!' Harriet exclaimed.

Clank went the burnished metal weight on the platform of the scale, the thud of yellowed apples – giant cookers – waxed-skinned pink grapefruit, blood oranges all coursing round the large eye-shaped metal bowl, the dry rustle of the brown paper bags setting Harriet's teeth on edge. At the snack van, next to a carnival of patterned dresses, a few slouchers queued for burgers and hot dogs, the singed grease foul in the air failing to register on their unmoved faces. Boredom was a shield for deeper feelings, you had to remember, but even still. One of the men was still bleeding slightly from last night's brawl. Above, the sky stretched pale like faded overalls.

Her mother had a modest cotton shirt-waister in that colour. She lived in Paris now and wore the wildly humble garment to help out in a day centre run by the American church. In the blue dress, and a sludge-green one just like it, she doled out soup and sandwiches to the deserving poor, organised appointments with the chiropodist and the outreach employment resettlement team. She was a sharp woman, endlessly critical and dismissive. She lived her life correcting and enduring in turn. The poor didn't deserve that, Harriet thought.

At the sweetie stand there was a scene of bewildering animation: shoving, whispers, hands darting into pockets, the flash of banknotes followed by hissed insults, cursing, recriminations. Were these hectic underhand transactions caused by sugar-love alone? Harriet rushed the girls past to more wholesome vistas.

In their festive cherry-checked smocks the girls skipped over the cobbles, linked at the hands like a chain of paper dolls. They were half drunk with glee, their limbs flailing, their hair blowing madly in the splendid wind, their jagged shrieks of mirth assaulting the flabby neighbouring birds. Clara, without thinking, unfurled the whole span of a joyous arm carelessly into Margot's head and you should have heard the yelps of ouch, the complaints, the pleas for justice and parents, the gaping mouths, even the wispy fringes and the lolling plaits railing for apologies and instant lollipop reparation. 'It's all right, it's all right, there's really no need to ...' Harriet cooed, patting and soothing and cheering and gathering in. She examined the scene before her zoologically for a moment. How they lived! All four seasons, all five senses and the elements and humours and dimensions sheer and stark in the space of three minutes. She loved the children for their animal incaution, the looseness of their carriage, their constant entreaties. There was none of the poignant adulteration that came in later life: the stoicism, the compromise, the dreaded *tact* – for every occurrence struck this species like a huge international disaster or its happy reverse.

'Four courgettes, please,' Harriet asked one of the stallholders.

'Hooray, a T. S. Eliot fan,' he countered, swinging the brown paper bag round by its ears.

'True,' she said. 'True.' Some days the world met your needs so acutely you would happily drop down dead on its behalf.

A young girl in unseasonable clothing joined the burger queue, unshy about the fall and rise of her blue-white midriff. Charles, the tramp from the corner, was out in full regalia, crumpled country trousers, frilled shirt and some kind of forlorn-looking tailcoat. The sun made a halo on his whiskery brow. He clasped an orange paperback of *The Iliad*. 'Good afternoon, sir', Harriet had the girls chorus. There was no other man in the world she would insist that they greet in such a way.

At the centre where her mother worked there were countless rules and regulations. A great deal was expected from the patrons for it was a 'dry' centre and there were regular tests for drugs and alcohol. You could even get into trouble, as a service-user, for letting slip, to a helper, a rogue '*chérie*'. Her mother was impressive to tackle such work. Consistent, doubt-free, quietly emphatic, there was something faultless now about her self-control. Harriet did not grate on her mother as she had once done. There was no longer any passion to their relation. They tried for cordial or, failing that, politeness and they sometimes attained it. It was a shrug that she provoked in her remaining parent, a dismissive sweeping gesture of the hand, uninterest, a blink, a blank.

An adolescent, shabby in colourless denim, was propped against some recycling bins murmuring very quietly to all passers-by, 'Skunk, weed, skunk, weed.'

'That's kind but no thank you very much.' Harriet's voice rang out with crispness and cheer. As a woman skirted by six small children you were infinitely powerful. Even squalor or mistreatment had no hold. She was phenomenal – completely vindicated and validated by her companions. The girls' heads bobbed up and down as they skipped along, each child maintaining a physical hold on her, a piece of her jacket fabric, a finger, a hand on her stockinged legs. They giggled at an underwear stall: enormous white lacy bras with cups the size of pudding basins, vast briefs hoisted up on hangers like surrender flags. The girls' high spirits escalated further, Harriet's rising to meet them.

'Hello, mum, how's about me rock-'ard tomarders, very fresh?' Mia trilled and all the other girls shook with so much laughter that Lily collapsed on the ground from it and Clara tripped over her knees, clutching Isabella's arm so that she went over too, and her long pink legs rudely splayed brought Flora down, for good measure, then Mia and Margot perched victorious atop the pile of them so that there were six little girls lying heaving with laughter, an hysterical multi-headed monster with twelve legs in frilled socks.

'Look!' Isabella cried, jumping to her feet as the street hushed, trading ceased, and the stallholders' loud patter died on their lips. Coming towards them on the pavement was a sort of visitation: six young girls in long, white, ghostly gowns embroidered with crystals or pearls, one covered in lace, another appliquéd with entwined doves. Shoulder-length veils covered their serious faces. They wore white shoes and two were carrying white satin drawstring purses. The smallest child had tights of white net with a complicated trellis of flower patterns in the threads. Leading them through the streets was a young priest in black robes, his fresh face luminous with hope. A clutch of greyish adults followed them at a remove.

From the market traders there came a smattering of applause as they passed.

'Is it a wedding for children?' Isabella asked.

'I think it's a First Communion,' Harriet said.

'What's that?'

'It's a ceremony in which Roman Catholic children receive a special sort of wafer biscuit from God, a biscuit of God, some people believe. You know God, the father of the Baby Jesus, have you heard of Him?'

'Oh yes.'

'Has Baby Jesus got any special biscuits for us?'

'Well . . .' Harriet said.

'We're doing meringues this afternoon with Serena,' said Flora.

'I always forget the vanilla,' Isabella murmured.

At home-time Harriet surveyed the huddle of parents gathering round the steps to her house from the front door spy-hole, hoping for clues. The bank of handsome fathers was especially impressive today, stylish and laconic, their clothing exquisitely distressed. They worked in television, these slouching, shrugging, sunglassed, freelance paps, or in advertising or pre- or post-production or music management or some other chaotic profitable underbelly of the vaguely creative arts.

Harriet threw open the front door and walked lightly down the steps. 'The girls are in the garden with Honey and Serena. They won't be more than a minute,' she said.

'Nat, Susannah's dad.' The fellow came forward, his hand like lettuce as he held it out to her.

'How do you do?' Harriet said, insisting he meet her gaze.

She looked hard at him, too hard she knew, and he was shaken by it. Something had been demanded and she saw him take the summons like a knock. They had no idea what to do with her, these gap-toothed, flailing thirty-something men who spoke haltingly with shy darting glances while deep down they brimmed with unalloyed self-regard. She brought them out in metaphorical hives and rashes. They could barely look her in the eye; they flushed, they stumbled, they became more straggly with each second. Marvellously uncanny, she disarmed them completely. A headmistress in the flesh, it was a great deal more embarrassment than they could take. But if everything about them expressed adroit evasions of commitment, she could hardly be expected to collude.

If you think I'm hard work you really ought to meet my ma, Harriet laughed to herself. She would reduce you all to mincemeat in a flash. The lively disapproval that poured out of her mother coloured everything; it lowered and hardened, reducing, limiting, rejecting. It was a substantially toxic pollutant, freezing all the good things out of of you until you were forced to put forward the very version of yourself she loathed.

Two mothers appeared, perfumed and leisurely, dazzling in their pale grey cashmere knitwear and their Hellmann's-coloured hair. They wore fine jewellery, heavy gem-studded gold decorative crosses, large-stoned rings; their mildly jaunty shoes and bags were humorous depositories for their pride. En masse such women might appal, but there wasn't a single one of her parents who wasn't trying to improve. Harriet had required it of them in the questions she had asked at interview. The school interiors charmed everyone immediately, but it wasn't just about the beguiling appearance of things. 'This is a school for people who believe the bringing up of children is the most important thing they'll ever do. If we mess that up, nothing else in life will mean very much. You'll notice in the prospectus I don't really care about academic standards at this stage. I could have them all writing perfect cursive script by the end of the year, but these aren't circus chimps. Childhood isn't a preparatory state, an antechamber to one's real life which can be bargained away in return for later gains. Like any other extended period, the aim must be to pass it in the happiest and most interesting way. Do you agree?'

Any mother and father who paused for more than half a second was summarily dispatched. 'I can be very "off with your heads",' Harriet smiled, as they left. But those who did agree expressed vast warmth towards her. A community based on great and mindful larks was what she invited them to join. There was an obvious appeal. It wasn't complicated.

Now Mia's father was telling some sort of story, something about a disastrously failing art show, losing tens of thousands, if such a thing were possible, and then Clara's father joined this little gathering, and he said something so dashing or naive it made each of the others shake his head, and there followed an orgy of sardonic looks.

More mothers arrived, whispering like conspirators. One, the leader, was in challenging, asymmetric costume with threads hanging and odd points and thrusts and gathers in her skirts where thrusts and gathers perhaps did not belong. Was it a hop picker she was hoping to emulate or some kind of émigré soothsayer? Her cohort was dressed in the style of a Sicilian widow with panels of black lace set into her thick navy dress, and tiny clumpy shoes. It was festive in the extreme this home-time wardrobe entertainment. It surely wasn't wrong to feel a prick of pride. Harriet looked, then looked again. Oh no! The woman who had just joined them, poured into green-flecked tweed, was sporting a large diamond pavé brooch on her lapel that bore in a pretty italic script the legend *Crack Whore*.

Harriet, grinning, decided a little speech was in order. 'Good afternoon, everyone' – straggly murmurs in response. 'These are wonderful and lovely children. Thank you for entrusting them into my care. We've had a marvellous week. I'm sure you've all heard a potted version of the highlights, one of which was the manufacture of our Tudor family, and then, of course, my being given a crash course in cartwheeling by some of the girls. I only wish there was time to demonstrate my new skills.' She gave a wryish smile and paused for the faint laughter. 'We are trying to make everything here completely playful, messy, exciting and when necessary sooth-ing, following the children's own interests completely. I want them to feel that absolutely anything's possible.'

One of the fathers, close-cropped hair, white face, huge embar-rassed smile and a body hanging lankly from his six-and-a-half-foot frame, sported a T-shirt that said *J' ♥ ta femme*. You couldn't deny it was chic.

'Now, are there any questions, or, er,' and she spoke the word as if it were the epitome of wild daring, '*complaints*? From three thirty every day I will always be available to speak to any parents with concerns about school life. We'll call it the unhappy hour. Would anyone like to see me now?' Silence. 'No? Good.' She would not pause for long.

She turned briskly, half wishing she had a cape to swish or some other garment conducive to a grand exit. She was just about to return to her top-floor flat and her tea and toast routine when—

'Excuse me? I'd like to talk to you about something?' Margot's mother stood tugging at the ugly ring she wore on her thumb. Harriet flinched at the woman's double up-speak (she was squeam-ish about what linguists called the high rising terminal) but it would be rough, she did see, to let this be known.

'Of course,' she said instead, ushering her into the ground-floor schoolroom, taking for herself the administrator's chair, showing the mother on to one of the girls' little rush-matted stools. Harriet sniffed loudly. The woman was wearing so much scent you could not help wondering what it was she wanted to hide.

'What it is, is' – the opening was also badly styled – 'it's just that looking at the paintings Margot has brought home from school this week I can't help noticing that she seems to be using many more cold colours in them than the warmer colours and I found myself wondering whether the warmer colours you know the oranges and reds and pinks' – Harriet nodded curtly – 'were as well represented in your paint pots because these are the colours she tends to use at home.' Harriet sniffed again; the woman had the effect of a mild chemical irritant.

'Would you like to inspect our art supplies cupboard or look at some of the other children's work?' Harriet put the question calmly. 'It might be reassuring.'

They climbed together the two flights of stairs. At the window on the landing, in the half-light, Harriet thought, I could put my arm through that pane of glass right now. She flexed her fingers and made a fist of her right hand. Yes, but that is exactly what people would expect, she countered.

In the art department, Harriet paused, markedly, in front of paintings of sunsets and fire engines and poppy fields. At each easel there were fourteen different pots of paint. With all these colours you instantly achieved more interesting work. (Harriet was proud of this, for most nurseries she had inspected offered each child only five or six shades at a time.)

Margot's mother looked puzzled. 'Perhaps she feels somehow that the atmosphere at school is a little cooler than the atmosphere at home.'

'Do you really think that?'

'What do you think?'

'Well, I suppose I think Margot has settled in well. We've noticed that she seems to love singing so we've really encouraged that and she's also really interested in the garden, so she's been out there a lot this week, helping Serena plant spring bulbs, and today she said she'd like to try her hand at a bit of woodwork . . .'

'She doesn't speak about school much, but then . . .'

'But then . . .'

'I don't know. Perhaps I'm just being hopeless.'

'Well, I wouldn't go that far.'

'Of course my husband loves the children . . .'

'I'm sure.' Harriet's eyes widened.

'But he has got a temper. Margot likes things to be calm and quiet, we all do, and I don't think she finds any of it easy.'

'No.'

'I really hate it actually.'

'Yes,' Harriet said. 'It must be—'

'I don't really know what to do.' The mother covered her face with her hands. 'I'm so sorry. You must think . . .'

'Please.' Harriet fished a box of bunny-print tissues from Linda's desk and placed it in her hands.

'Thanks. Oh dear, this isn't what I planned. I'm so embarrassed.'

'Please don't be. I of all people—' Harriet stopped. She was old pals with embarrassment now – she practically fed it and clothed it – but she needn't disclose her flaws to virtual strangers. 'Everyone finds a child's transition to nursery extremely taxing.'

She formed a delicate question in her head. But there's just a little something I find I need to ask you, so, when you speak of your husband's temper I'm wondering if – ah – I'd be very far-fetched in wondering whether perhaps outbursts of violence are also an aspect of this temper of his or whether . . . whether that's not really a concern that – ah – needs addressing? But she did not put these words to her assailant. There was only so far you could, at first, go.

The mother was gazing silently at the paintings that were tacked to the wall with red drawing pins.

'I was at art school when I was younger.'

Harriet nodded. 'Oh really?'

'I wanted to be a sculptor, but I didn't have the confidence.'

'What kind of medium did you work in?'

'Oh, it never really got that far. My parents didn't support me. They thought I was – they didn't take me at all seriously about anything.'

'What a shame. How awful. I am sorry.'

'It was a long time ago.'

Harriet showed the mother off the school premises. The woman evidently loathed herself – that was hardly unusual – but how could people live without pride? She softened herself deliberately. Should she offer in some light way to assist with the angry husband? There were courses one could do. Could the mother be encouraged to resume her study of sculpture, at this late stage? It might mean the world.

The plain fact was that if your parents weren't interested or your brother or sister or even your enemy's dog, you simply had to look elsewhere for what you sought. She had written to both her relations the quietest of postcards letting them know about her school, and of course received a large fat zero by return of post. You could waste your life putting yourself in their way in the most flattering light, showing off your best side, relentlessly doling out the most thoughtful gifts and the sunniest greetings cards, but when nothing ever came back? Should you keep on dragging your body in front of the firing squad, only to be – and why this was such a colossal insult she did not know – ignored?

Without warning Harriet recalled the thin features of a man she'd been involved with – it was wall-to-wall misery, years ago, never mind – and remembered how his face had finally lit with love at the moment they had finished things and he said with peace and passion, 'You mean I'm free to go?' She thought of another man, an antiquarian bookseller, telling her, 'Somebody hurt you once and you've never forgiven everyone.'

And then there was her brother, nearly four years older, stern and disapproving in his naval uniform and single medal, excruciated by the merest thing about her. There was never a mistake, for him, which she failed to make. Her height for instance, the size of her feet, embarrassed him acutely. He found her general high colour (the red-gold hair, the rough pink cheeks) alarming and was always attempting to turn down the brightness of her and the tone. But he held it, all of it – to her mind – so incorrectly. For never once did Harriet, as he thought she did, look at her limbs and see angelic rose-bloom lacework on a luxurious scale; no, she minded her own coarse raddishy flush and blotches long before he ever did, and with more passion.

Five years ago he had told her, with finality, that she was a very angry person and that he was made uncomfortable by this, as was his silent wife. They did not want to see her any more. He said it softly. There was half a minute of mutual gaze. To say something nasty in a kindish voice, what was the meaning of it? Was it some sort of joke? Colin looked at her more gravely and then with derision. Only she, of all people, would be capable of such warped interpretation. His strength of feeling was utterly startling. It did not make him the smallest bit grand, but for this greyish half-man it was a sort of distinction. The meaning was clear then. All the air flew from the room. She hid her hurt, of course, nodding quietly and retreating. She apologised softly, walking backwards out of his front door, stumbling over his sun-drenched front lawn, which was lavish with daisies.

She could parody her own manner better than anyone else, she wanted to tell him: the crimson self-command, the rigorous flights of fancy, the grating hesitancies grown in the suspicion that she was overbearing. But it wasn't true she was the type who dedicated her whole life to exacting satisfaction for some perceived wrong. That was just his excuse. She had no value in his eyes and now he had thrown her away.

She double-locked the front door against further mad petitioners and took herself off to the upper floor. And, you know, perhaps with my mother it's simply nothing more than a personality clash, she explained it away to herself evenly, as she mounted the broad stairs.

Coiled safely in her red velvet chair she thought of the trip back to London on the Eurostar, after the last disastrous visit to her mother two years ago. Even Paris had loathed her! The looks of horror on the faces of the women in the shoe shops. '*Quarante-trois italienne!*' To win Paris over she would need to stretch her womanhood to the brink of effeminacy, employ the navy blue smouldering of a seasoned femme fatale. Well, she wouldn't do it. She couldn't do it. On the train home she was eating some very ripe cheese, some shards of cracker, apple parings, piecing things together. She saw things clearly and calmly for once. The soft things in me make my mother harden. The strong things in me offend her taste. If we were not related perhaps then it wouldn't even . . . and she does try for politeness, but it's the sort of politeness you use with a stranger on an ill-lit street at night in a bad neighbourhood. It's brutal. It's self-defence.

The train had been crammed with romantic holiday-takers finger-feeding each other salted cashews and green olives with lingering looks. A ragged school party was sweating contraband cider while a table of four businessmen, suits straining at their lunches, surveyed the shimmering schoolgirls with monstrous intent. And all around the scent of dingy stain-resistant carriage cloth. Harriet's spirits sank then sank again. She went to the buffet car and bought a quarter-bottle of champagne, just to show everybody. She did not like champagne particularly but felt it represented a certain flamboyant abandon. She filled a plastic flute and clinked it dully against the side of the table, mouthing, 'Cheers, me dears.'

She had thought of her brother as she drank. She thought of her sister-in-law, Maggie. They have simply cast me in a drama that has nothing at all to do with who I am. She shook her head. A ridiculous pair. Their idea of bliss was being on a cruise whiling away hours at deck quoits. They were even more lifeless than the couple in their weather clock, who at least reacted to external circumstances.

She did not believe they were unhappy. To them unhappiness, like shyness, was a moral failure. Even sneezing was a bodily function worthy of disdain. How they had ever produced children. The children were lovely, Robin and Caroline, that was the one thing that didn't quite add up; warm and excitable little cuckoos in the ice nest. The boy with his pinkish, shy laugh, the girl breathless and high-spirited, permanently chattering.

She felt indulgent towards her brother and sister-in-law

40

suddenly. Really, they were babies. She took another sip from her plastic glass. They were fifteen minutes from St Pancras now and she gathered her lumpy belongings and piled them on to her lap. If your father prized reticence above all human traits the chances of your brother being effusive were awfully slim. She did see that. It would be like mastering a language that you'd never heard in your life.

At her brother's wedding, her father stood expressionless in *his* father's fine tailcoat, jabbing his jagged keys into the whites of his palms. He's going to draw blood, Harriet thought. Drips of blood down the front of the order of service! She willed her mother to stop him, but her mother seemed to think it none of her concern. 'Their trouble is they are just too similar,' she had said to Harriet once, and on another occasion, 'They're too different, that's all it is.'

The congregation was small. Colin's college friends were even more strained-looking than he. Was it possible he was the relaxed one of their group? Harriet stood alone; she had asked if she might bring a friend but they said, 'Oh, you see the numbers ...'

Her boyfriend at the time had thought the prohibition came from her. 'Worry I'll use the wrong spoon?' Dave had muttered. He was a teacher in a primary school who spoke his mind.

'Of course not,' she had answered. 'It's just not going to be much of a party. These people are not what you'd call fun.' But the dinner afterwards in the hotel had been very grand. There had been swans made of ice filled with caviar. (She hadn't told him that.)

'So holy, so dignified,' one of the bride's aunts said to the other one, spritzing her wrists with perfume from a cut-glass atomiser in the hotel Ladies. An attendant in black dress and white organdie apron was folding linen huck towels. The carpet had raspberry-coloured roses and green leaves woven into the design. Harriet, hidden by a column of pink marble, held her breath.

'Maggie needs some good luck,' the other said, 'and you know he proposed the very first time he took her out? He had made up his mind and that was that.'

'No! And what did Maggie say?'

'Well, they were sitting in the restaurant, I think they had finished their mains and he took up her hand and just asked her out of the blue. Hadn't even ordered their desserts.'

'And what did she say?'

'Well, she said ask me again a year from today and I will say yes.'

'Sensible.'

'Yes, but friendly too.'

'And was there a ring then, or not at that stage?'

'He took her out to choose one the following day, antique, three-stone, from the Burlington Arcade.'

'Very nice. And then, sorry to ask, did they order a dessert or did they leave it there?'

'No, no, they went the whole hog, I'm sure. You would on a night like that. Well, I say that but more than likely it was something fruit based because they neither of them like to over-indulge.'

Harriet emerged and loitered at the basins, avoiding her reflection in the mirror. Her dress could have done with being more sedate.

'Hello, dear,' the aunts said in unison.

'Oh, hello.' She smiled. 'Are you having a lovely time?'

'You'll be next,' they said and her cheeks went the colour of the roses in the carpet.

*

When the Paris train drew into the echoing station, coats and bags and cases were pulled roughly from the racks. Harriet held her seat until the carriage was empty. There was no rush, she did not have to be anywhere in particular, but the cleaners were on board now sweeping armfuls of rubbish into large clear plastic sacks. Still she did not move. She was getting looks. What are you even doing? She shook her head. Sometimes she dreamed that her mother and brother lay side by side in her parents' bed at home with the blue wallpaper. It was passionless, a laughable scene – they were bickering over who had the lion's share of the duvet. Her brother wore grey pyjamas with white piping and sharp creases. Her mother's shoulders were draped in a thick shawl. It was morning and her brother picked up a newspaper and fenced himself off with it. Her mother took up her knitting needles. Their day clothes lay neatly folded on a chair in the corner of the room, their shoes tucked out of sight. Even their incest was petty and banal. What could you do?

The only really important thing was that you did not blame yourself, she thought, clambering off the train, traipsing inelegantly up the platform, smears of cheese on her blouse, skirts tangling in the wheels of her small rolling valise.

A candid ring on the front door bell and Harriet sprang out of her red chair and raced down the three flights to the front hall and there at the threshold stood Clementine's father, so tightly furled in dark business attire he appeared to be impersonating an umbrella. You had to feel sorry for him.

'Hello, yes, look,' he began, and then, 'No thanks, I'd rather stand' to the small proffered chair.

Is it a fight he's looking for? Harriet rose grandly. Good. *Bring It On* by Miss Harriet Irene Mansfield.

'I am not happy about the way Clementine was spoken to by a member of your staff yesterday afternoon.'

'Oh? I'm very sorry to hear that. Would you expand?'

'Whether it's because your assistants were distracted or dropped their guard or whatever – I simply don't want Clementine being dealt with in that way.'

'Yes?'

'I am talking about the ridiculous amount of praise being doled out in this school. Example: one of your assistants saw a feeble drawing Clemmie did and said, "Oh, Clemmie, that's just *so* lovely and amazing. Wow. You're quite the artist!" et cetera et cetera and I have to say that I don't want her on the receiving end of that kind of communication. It's utterly meaningless.'

'But could you not—'

'Let me finish *please*. If her every scribble is greeted like an important masterpiece . . . I gather your intention is to be encouraging and character- and confidence-building, but that is not the way to go about it. If your assistants were to say "Goodness you have used a great deal of yellow which makes the hay look very fresh" it could have led to an interesting discussion about the saturation of colour that some things in nature have. I don't want Clemmie being exposed to mindless praise. Children know when they are being fobbed off.'

'Indeed. But may I ask you something? Are you referring to the extraordinary picture of the hayfield that she did, with the farmer and the fruit trees and the cattle grazing near the blue lake, with hills in the distance?'

'I can't remember exactly. It may have been something vaguely pastoral, yes.'

'I take your point about mindless praise. It is not something we go in for here at all, so demoralising. But what you are ignoring is that the picture Clementine did was really exceptional. Our raptures were genuine. I mean the composition was awfully well judged and the amount of feeling she conveyed in the figures, even in the animals, was an extraordinary achievement, we thought, in one so young. There was a sad resigned look on the calf that was being led away from its mother and there was something in the set of the hills that seemed to suggest, in a kind of pathetic fallacy, that they were feeling the adult animal's sadness. We almost wondered if the work wasn't a sort of veiled commentary on the experience of beginning school for the first time, from the perspective of both child and parent. The painting is at the framer's now, I took it round last night, there's one just beyond the market that's very good, so perhaps what I'm really saying is that rather than our overestimating, you may be guilty of an underestimation yourself. Not that I wish to criticise or find fault. But to call it a scribble . . . '

'Ah,' the father said. 'Ah, well, but you will, please, be more careful in future when you speak to Clemmie.'

'I beg your pardon?'

Oh please please please can I let him have it? Harriet begged herself – *Burning My Boats* by H. I. Mansfield, vols 1–14, morocco bound – but the permission for an outburst would not come. No, she said under her breath, not. Come on! But if she could only meet him with a long look and a 'Sir! You must agree your comments are highly eccentric. I know you work in the financial sector and this is off the top of my head, of course, but I wonder if you see little value in artistic achievement or are threatened or made uncomfortable by it or feel a sort of latent hostility in relation to it because it isn't quite of your own sphere? Because your own talents are somehow less ... or rather more ... not conventional, not squalid exactly, I don't quite mean that but – yes, actually I do.'

You never ever let me have any fun! she complained to herself, wry, theatrical. Oh the pleasure you could have in life, if you gave yourself full rein ...

Instead: 'Apologies if what I've said was a little strong. I do think very open communication terribly valuable and thank you for your comments. And from what you've outlined about your attitudes towards conversation I felt it correct to be exact and frank. Will you excuse me now? You see I've a meeting about Harvest Festival celebrations in a moment. I'm thinking of squash and gourd, snow-berries, Japanese anemones, last of the garden roses, masses of foliage red and green, little baskets of marzipan fruit everywhere, and then ... Terribly exciting! But do please keep in touch. We do so value your imput.'

The father, in a state of mild confusion, was descending the steps to the black and white tiles, rubbing the side of his head.

'Naughty!' Harriet said, giving herself a very light rap on the knuckles. The painting she had described, the one at the framer's with the pathetic hills and mournful livestock, the blue lake and the intensely lush green pasture, had been an instant artwork of her own imagination. *It did not exist.* But honestly. That disgusting English thing of doing your children down all the time – it was, of course, one of the commoner branches of sadism, but even still. 'I will not tolerate it in my school,' she murmured with a sharp little cry of joy. 'I will not tolerate it in my life.'

Even in the auction rooms on that greyish January day when the occasional burst of light through the high windows was so sharp you could not help but think of breakages, even when the star attraction appeared, the original 1930s gypsy wagonette, and every child present was vowing to its mother undying love for evermore, as well as uninterrupted table laying and bed making and times table recitations, unadulterated pure goodness and sweetie discipline until death, and even beyond, in return for the winning bid, Harriet would not blame herself. Not herself, not Flora who had been her undoing, or so the headlines had it. Not Sophie who could scarcely be held responsible, not her parents and certainly not her poor brother. Dear little Flora who would not have meant to hurt a fly. No one's intentions were bad, and that was always key.

In her rickety wooden chair at the auction Harriet gasped at the sight of the bright overblown roses painted on the stunning vehicle, the strong green lustre of the tow-bar, the retractable yellow steps and the little dotted Swiss curtains made to flutter at the windows in the breeze. It was important to know that all human people – with mixed results, it was true – were almost always doing the best they could. I know I am, she murmured.

Not in a Million Years

On Friday afternoon, when the house emptied of girls, the young staff prepared to leave, slightly raucous and dishevelled, prinking and preening in the downstairs lavatories for an early evening sortie to the West End shops.

Lingering before the low bank of miniature basins, slowly rinsing her hands, Harriet heard them chatting unguardedly inside the cubicles from their little red loo seats. She coughed lightly; she was not a spy. Serena said, 'Did you hear Mia? Hilarious! Saw her mum and dad kiss each other on the black and white tiles and said, "Look guys, I'd rather you got divorced than did that."'

'Oh no,' Harriet groaned with merriment.

'What time shall I pick you up tonight, Linda?' Tina said through the cubicle walls.

'Do I have to?' Linda answered from within. 'I was planning to catch up on my soaps.'

Tina made a growling noise. 'Unbelievable! How you going to meet someone if you stay in every night?'

Linda began remonstrating good-naturedly. She was wearing a new salmon-coloured Fair Isle cardigan today.

Tina said, 'Fingers in my ears, la la la.'

'All right, all right.' Linda caved in with humorous frustration. 'I surrender.'

'Good girl. And dancing is good for you, anyway. I'll call for you at nine. Can one of you guys pass me some loo paper under the thing,' Tina said. 'There's none in here.' A rustling sound. 'Oh, thanks.'

'Is the dance place you go to local?' Harriet called to them from the other side of the doors, just as Honey emerged and studied her reflection in the mirror. There was so much mute panic suddenly that Harriet corrected herself straight away. 'Of course, my dancing days are long behind me now.' Honey unfroze and began applying lilac, then pea-green, shimmer shadow to her eyelids.

Serena came out, rinsed her hands, dried them on her thighs then bent right over so her glossy chestnut hair hung down in a thick curtain over the front of her knees and started brushing it vigorously on the underside. Twenty strokes, Harriet counted, thirty-four. It was practically a Degas painting. Serena tossed her head back and began smoothing down the wild and lively mane. The air crackled with static and a tiny white particle from her scalp landed like a snowflake on Harriet's wrist. 'I'm going home tomorrow morning. Hooray! Dying to see everyone. Especially Mr Waffles.'

'Mr Waffles?' Honey shrieked.

'My horse! Don't laugh. I didn't name him myself.'

'I got off lightly with Honey,' Honey said. 'My sisters are Moonbeam and Starlight. It's normal in Totnes.'

Peals of laughter from Tina still inside the cubicle.

'Hilarious,' Serena said.

There followed what was unmistakably Tina's prolonged stream of urine. They all avoided each other's gaze and pretended not to hear. Then a *plop!* Harriet bit her lip. A faint smell of meat and coffee rose up. 'I'm planning to spend the weekend with my boys,' Honey said quickly. The boys were Eggs and Bacon, the dogs from the illustrated children's story she was writing.

The sound of flushing and then Tina emerged, washed her hands and began applying mascara to her lashes with a frown-shaped wand. She stopped and started tapping the phial against the edge of the sink.

'Borrow mine,' Serena said. 'In fact, have it. I haven't opened it yet; it was two for one.'

Harriet breathed deeply and happily.

Serena drew out a flowery make-up case and began applying a wine-coloured lip pencil to Linda, very carefully through squinting eyes. Then she painted in the lipstick, taking a tiny brush to a dark red shiny column in a gold tube.

'Just don't make me look like a drag queen, okay?'

'This one's called Aristo-Claret,' Serena said.

Tina packed her cosmetics back into a small black purse. 'This is Starter Bride.' She inclined her head and peered at herself in the mirror. 'How do I look?'

'Perfect,' Harriet beamed, making with her open palm a curvaceous appraising arc. 'All of you. Confident, dashing, beautiful, but all these things very much by accident and not design, as though it just can't be helped.'

Tina giggled. Serena rolled her eyes but not with disrespect. Honey raised her shoulders and placed one hand across her breast, like an ardent heroine from a silent film. Linda went all over the colour of cherries.

This thriving chorus-girls backstage life was such a nutritious development! Should she fetch some wine? A lavatory party: could anything *be* more jolly? And really it was only half not true.

It was time for the staff to leave. 'Thanks so much for everything you've done this week,' Harriet called through the door. 'You're wonderful, all of you. I don't think things could really be better!' But they had already passed through the building, primed for festivity. She picked up a dirty cotton bud and a lipsticked tissue and placed them in the pedal bin. She wiped the lip of the basin where a dusting of silver powder had collected.

By four fifteen when the building was utterly empty, the house began to fail slightly and with it Harriet. The school, flooded with lifelessness, was mocking her faintly and this was especially harsh as she had assumed, for some reason, it would take her side. The rooms looked despairing in the light of such abandonment: antiseptic, menacing. The hollowness of the playing room met her with rebukes, like a caustic sibling for whom she meant only trouble. 'What now?' – its challenge too direct for comfort.

Harriet went down to the stationery cupboard in the basement, ran her fingers along shelves neatly stacked with drawing books and writing books, nodded at boxes of pencils and markers and sharpeners and rubbers, a tray of scissors, card stock, sticky labels, glue sticks, a ream of sugar paper, squares of felt in rainbow hues. She uncapped a highlighter pen and wrote her initials on the palm of her hand. She inhaled the dry woody odour of order and plenty, thinking, thinking. You *cannot* let the heart seep out of you every time the weekend comes.

Yet it was a callous hour and it was hard for there not to spread through Harriet a terribly sharp— But she wouldn't allow it, not for a moment; she was braced for such onslaughts. She forbade such indulgences. *You Have a Choice* by Harriet Mansfield.

'Are you afraid you may be heading for a breakdown?' medics had asked her on more than one occasion, a psychiatrist with sea-green eyes when she was eighteen, a nurse with bleached blonde hair when she was twenty-three, a GP who had an embroidered picture in his consulting room that said *The Lord Will Heal* – not terribly reassuring, that. And once or twice Miss McGee.

'It won't happen without my permission,' she had said the first time. She laughed ruefully at the thought of this sanguine pronouncement. She had a diary in an upstairs drawer that proved you could not legislate on these matters, her high spirits and her courage veering swiftly downhill on the page. Yet she wouldn't meet the early evening undefended. She must draw on contingency reserves.

She crept again up to the first-floor playing room, half hoping for improvement, but the room was so live with missing persons it was like a crime scene. She had willpower in great swathes, however. You will not fail yourself, she said. She forced herself to read a fashionable new American novel, with a tight smile, for a whole hour before finally throwing it down sighing, Where are the characters, where are the feelings?

She went up to her floor, paused by the mantelpiece and dropped an aspirin into a vase of drooping lilies. She caught her face in the mirror looking quite cheerful in a miserable sort of way. If 'Grin and Bear It' were a chapter in a book she could write in her sleep, it did not mean she was a bad person. The neighbour's house was leaking complex orchestral sounds and she blinked hard: if things seemed momentarily vacant it was, on the whole, an exciting time. She lay down on her rug and coiled her limbs almost affectionately, gazing through the window at the wet silk light. She imagined Flora in a hotel tea room with her psychoanalyst father.

'Are you having a happy childhood?' he would ask from time to time. Offering a plate of sticky cakes, she saw him, or handing round a stack of finger sandwiches, pouring daringly for his daughter a weak warm cup of tea. Might Harriet join them if she by chance were passing? 'Be our guest!' Would they colour in the afternoon together, scheming delicious little schemes? *The Art of Consolation* all the three? She dozed for a moment until she heard the clatter of the letter box – post! – and raced down to retrieve it, half knowing it was only the pizza deliverer's multicoloured flyer, the local window cleaner's plea for an extra home: 'Your pane is our gain.'

A letter in a thick white envelope awaited her. It was from Margot's mother. They were withdrawing Margot from the school! Harriet sat down, knocking her hip against the fireplace roughly, headed paper quivering in her hand. They were thinking of moving to the country, they claimed. It was nothing against the school, the letter stressed, but there was something in the tone. They conceded grudgingly that they would pay the term's fees in accordance with the agreement they had signed. And this had been decided in a matter of days? She dialled Margot's house but an answering service clicked on and a stage-managed child's voice uttered, excruciatingly, 'I'm thorry but Mummy can't come to the phone, pleathe leave a methage after the beepy thing.' She let the phone fall in her arms. And, really, what would she have said? And then there were seventeen?

She walked out of the house into the dusky ruins of the market, stepping over crates of pitted fruit and ragged lettuces. Charles was sitting, not without dignity, on the pavement outside Drinkers Paradise. 'Good evening,' he said.

She put a hand to her unkempt hair and nodded and coloured

and smiled. He was climbing to his feet for her, a long shuffling process. Beneath some knotted blankets his crumpled trousers were held with string and he wore an ancient white shirt beneath a fisherman's jersey and over the top a dark green evening jacket with satin lapels. Haggard now, it must once have been really something.

'Beautiful coat!' she blurted. 'I wish I had a top hat for you.'

He smiled, but it was well controlled. 'Look, I've never been one for that kind of talk', she almost seemed to hear him say.

He was quite close to her now, close enough for her to slip her arm through his, not that in a million years she would ever— But he had other ideas. He took a spiral corkscrew to a bottle of Rioja and she took it as her cue to go away. In the brown pub opposite she sat at a corner table for half an hour, nursing a glass of watery whisky, vaguely hoping. If someone tried to sell her drugs now she might very well comply. A man came and sat with her, running his nail down the seam of a packet of crisps and opening up the greasy whole. She pulled herself up very straight. His neat beard and horn-rimmed glasses lent an intellectual air. He stood to order a plate of sausage sandwiches; he worked in pornography, he said.

'Oh?' she said. 'Is that, is that interesting?'

'Not really,' he replied and a few minutes after that they went their separate ways.

How very lovely! Harvest Festival! Harriet rallied at dawn on Sunday morning, rising from a fifteen-hour sleep, her head clouded and thick as though a bucket of silt had been poured between her jaw and her scalp. That was three sleeping pills for you. She ought not to take them but what was she meant to do? She made an elaborate kedgeree (*Be Kind! Be Kind! Be Kind!* by Harriet Mansfield) then still eggy, still ricy and fishy she plundered the park for decorations. The light was dazzling and the thin rain on her face was fresh and clean. A flurry of autumn leaves blew towards her and nested in her hair. Pride was red in her cheeks, pride was caked in muddy clumps to her skirts as she filled her arms with fallen crackling branches and acorns and glossy conkers and green-yellow-red-brown foliage. She walked her cargo home, carrying large portions of old tree across herself, as though it were a hero lying in her arms.

Then, in the school basement kitchen, working egg yolks into sugar and powdered almonds and almond essence, Harriet produced without a hint of sweat six pounds of soft almond paste. She set about the bold manufacture of several hundred subtly tinted miniature marzipan fruits to fill a small basket for each of her girls. She painted quick brown lines down curved bodies of bananas, she inserted cloves into blushing strawberries' clefts. She drew white streaks on limes and lemons to show exactly where they hit the light. God is in the detail, she thought vaguely. Or is it the devil? Her produce grew by gradual degrees. Her sugar fruit factory flourished. Hours passed and her arms grew tired but she was happyish in the knowledge that she was gainfully employed on behalf of the next generation, although *Killing Time with Confectionery* was not a book she would deign to write any time soon.

Seven hours into this process the pleasing artistic endeavour betrayed her, revealing itself to be little more than heavy drudgery. Her marzipan headache, like the sort that came with eating ice cream too fast, mocked her, and her wrists, which were tarred and feathered with egg yolk and powdered nuts, sent a florescent stinging rash up her arms. She laboured against the clock. Almond poisoning it would say in the coroner's report.

At two o'clock on Monday morning Harriet was *still* knee-deep in marzipan. I have been doing this for eleven hours! she cursed. She was so tired she was seeing withered yellow threads in the air. She had staying power, certainly, but where had all the pleasure gone? She took a swig from a pint mug of cold coffee. The playing room was now decked out in sheaves of corn and massive branches studded with birds' nests and garlands of fruit and flowers, the mantelpieces decorated with gourds and squash, blackberry briars from the garden and the last of the old white roses clustered in jam jars. Piles of ripe apples, red and pale gold, and pine cones and horse chestnuts were intertwined with ivy and snowberries and dark green leaves and rosemary and mint and aniseed-scented fennel fronds. If you go in for that sort of thing, she sniffed.

How could she have known that if the fruit were to look realistic, each small basket would take the best part of an hour? She would be finished by eight fifteen if she did not go to bed at all, just in time to wash and breakfast before the girls arrived on Monday morning. 'Harvest cunting Festival.' She spoke the words out evenly. You couldn't make it up. Then, 'Why is no one ever, ever, helping me?' she cried into the sugary air.

Her aloneness dismayed her although, being brave, she barred such thoughts. She had almost had a daughter for a spell. She was the teenage child of the man Harriet still half loved. Jim, he was called, the man, Jim Rathbone Jones. If Daisy were here, this task would be funny. She was awfully dark. They could have rolled their eyes together. 'Who's the nutbag in charge of this evil occupational therapy wing!' Not that she and Daisy had been exactly thick . . .

For Daisy's father Harriet transformed herself completely. As an automatic romantic courtesy she laced herself in, pruned herself back. She sanded down her sharper attitudes. And she did other things: appearing before him shoeless in the main as he was four and a half inches shorter than she was and he was sore about it. 'Please don't mind,' Harriet cajoled. 'It's charming, it's lucky, like suddenly realising halfway through the day that your jersey is inside out.'

In his company the acute relentless thoughts, the aches, the ancient, mindless games of blame and grief simply fell away. He felt such warmth towards her she went days in a row immune to her family. Even the pavements, the paving stones themselves that could seem so harsh and cold and, well, *sardonic* when she walked alone behaved themselves when Jim was with her. She had pictured them occasionally in a strange conditional future tense, naked with emotion at the altar of a church. She saw a house with a green dresser.

She was softened and lightly smiling almost always then, cultivating a sort of quiet stillness in herself which she believed he found feminine in the extreme. She rather liked it herself. It was the plainest form of fancy dress, the shepherdess or the kitchen maid. When they rose from his bed she took care to smooth the ecstatic disarray of her hair. She dropped no rapid, dismaying, nervous remarks. Instead she spoke carefully – he hated it when people exaggerated, it seemed to him the lowest kind of lie. The things he minded! 'But everything about me's exaggerated and overblown,' she whispered into his pillow as he slept. 'I'm a sort of caricature,' she confided to the damp and powdery linen which cushioned his beautiful king-shrimp ear. 'I'm big, garish, I'm overt. When I'm in a car with people they wind their windows down to let a bit of me out!' She shook her head ruefully but she was smiling. 'Why have you picked the wrongest possible type?' Yet he didn't seem to notice what was wrong with her or, if he did, he didn't mind. He brought her presents all the time, inspired ones: arriving at her door one evening bearing a large lead window box ready planted with a herb garden; a gigantic striped scarf the very week the weather turned; and then, on her birthday, a tiny emerald set in seed pearls on a delicate gold chain that she wore night and day.

She had been four years without sex, so in their erotic life she allowed herself to be a vehement gymnast, when it was dark. Perhaps I cannot help it, she thought. For who knew how long the romance might last? They eked out each night with sleep playing little or no part. The man even remarked upon it. 'You're very different,' he said thoughtfully, 'in the night from in the day. That's not a criticism, by the way. In fact you may take it as a compliment.'

'We're a huge success!' Harriet thought.

Daisy, the daughter at boarding school, was nearly fifteen. One Sunday they drove down to Sussex together and took her out for tea. The waitresses wore floor-length white aprons over fresh green gowns and the countless pairs of antique sugar tongs mounted on the walls in box frames looked like instruments of mild torture.

Daisy was sullen and uncommunicative, shredding then crushing in her fist a series of innocent doilies. They all watched themselves inverted in the gleaming silver teapot's cheek. Jim, at a loss, took himself off to the Gents. Daisy started to cry. She sobbed mascara and hide-the-blemish into Harriet's lilac silk satin blouse. Her frame was minuscule in Harriet's arms but there was nothing childish about her crying which was adult and heavy. Between them now was a fierce bond of mucus and hot tears and stray bits of hair and raspberry pips and caught breath and dribbles of saliva and crumbs and clotted cream and raisin pulp.

Jim returned but hung back from the vivid women's scene. He nodded encouragingly at Harriet and busied himself at the side of the shop where a small display cabinet was filled with frail china and glass for sale. Afterwards there was a stream of compliments that left Harriet shimmering.

A few days later Daisy arrived on Harriet's doorstep in the dead of night. She was awfully theatrical in her way. 'Please don't tell my father that I'm here.'

'The school will be worried about you.'

'They won't notice until morning that I've gone.'

'I must ring your father.'

'He'll make me go back.'

'Not if you tell him what the matter is.'

'He won't understand.'

'He might. You should try him.'

'Could I tell you and you tell him?'

'All right. But first I must ring and let him know you're safe.'

Harriet came back into the sitting-room. 'I haven't even offered you something to eat,' she said. They sat together arm in arm on the sofa. Then Daisy stretched out and flopped her head on Harriet's knee and Harriet stroked very very delicately her lovely dark blonde hair.

'First of all I want to thank you for making my father so happy. And he is happy. Obviously you don't know what he was like before you met but he is a different man.' Daisy spoke formally, but her voice for all its coolness was uncertain.

'Different in what way?'

'After my mother died, he sank very low. He was drinking a lot. I was very worried about him. They were very close, perhaps too close. They didn't see the need for anyone else. It was,' she cleared

59

her throat, 'a story-book romance. My mother's illness destroyed her but it destroyed him too. He had these awful night terrors. He'd wake up screaming like a mad person. He wouldn't stop shaking. His face was completely out of control. It was like a fit. He'd take hours to recover. I had to hold him. He was terrified, shaking, moaning. We went to the doctor's about it, he didn't want to go but I didn't know what else to try.'

'What did the doctor say?'

'That it was, kind of, an extreme bereavement reaction. Then I came home from school in the holidays and there was all this white transparent flakes of stuff everywhere and I couldn't think what it was. It was terrible, like animal scales or the skin of insects after they've turned into moths or whatever, totally gross, and I thought there was some kind of infestation and I phoned the council but then I saw that it was just falling off his hands, falling on the ground, off his neck, his arms. It was his skin. We went back to the doctor and the doctor said he'd once heard of it happening before. The body experiencing such terrible grief that it literally started falling apart.'

Harriet sat back in her chair, assuming the posture of one who relaxed.

'He wasn't eating at all then. He lost so much weight that he could fit into Mummy's jumpers. And she was really petite, you know, fine-boned, like me. He wore them like all the time, stopped washing, started to stink. Didn't want to wash her smell off him. I thought he was going to kill himself because he started giving a lot of his things away. I phoned the Samaritans when I had to go back to school and asked if they could ring him in the evenings sometimes to check up but they said it didn't work like that. They said he had to make the call. I threw all the paracetamol out of the medical box and hid the knives. It was pathetic but that's all I could think of. My marks were terrible at school and the teachers came down on me like a ton of bricks.'

'That was harsh of them,' Harriet interjected.

'I know but they said at these times it was just as possible to throw yourself into your work as to neglect it and they thought me being usually so conscientious and coming top and everything that I'd lose my whole identity if I started failing. Then there was this chemistry teacher at school who was really into me.'

'Romantically, you mean?'

'Well, I don't know about that, but we had sex a few times at night in the gym – he had a key.'

'But that's – that's appalling.'

'It wasn't great.'

'Does your father know about this?'

'No, and you promised you wouldn't tell him either.'

'I haven't promised that.'

'It's . . . it's not true anyway. I made it up.'

'Daisy, I think we should both get some sleep and talk more in the morning. Would that be all right?'

'Will you promise me something, just one thing and then I'll go to bed?'

'What's that?'

'I want you to leave us alone.'

'Go away, you mean?'

'Leave Dad and me. We're fine. We really don't need—'

'We'll talk about it in the morning, shall we?'

'Look, I've just lost my mother, am I going to lose my father as well?'

'Well, I don't know what to say. It's – well. For me it's very serious. It's a sort of crisis, falling in love, a good crisis but a crisis none the less. I don't know if you can understand. It's not something I'm good at, being loved by other people. Most people, especially those who know me best, don't like me.' She laughed, but the sound she made was ugly. 'My family and so on. I don't know how to explain exactly but it's an enormous life event for me, falling in love with your father. It's sort of an epiphany.'

'I don't want you to get hurt either. You're a lovely person but you seem all wrong for each other. You look so odd together. I don't know what your type is but you hardly let yourself breathe around him. It's like you're trying to be someone else.'

'All I can say is that I'm taking what you say very seriously. I'm going to give it a lot of thought.'

Harriet looked at Daisy tenderly, as the child's words pushed through her own crust of pain. Did you ever really love me, Harriet tried to piece the thing together, or did you make me think you did so I'd let you throw me away?

The following day the three of them ate spaghetti in a modern Italian café. Jim was attentive. 'Harriet, darling, is the light in your eyes?' 'Will you choose some wine?' 'I can't believe they haven't brought your pepper. Waiter! Waiter!'

She wanted to hit him. She regretted everything about herself, suddenly, from her uneven feelings to her tomato-coloured hair. Daisy merely referred to exam pressure, fierce competition among the girls, tragic teachers, some costly boots she wanted. ('May I buy them for you?' Harriet blurted.) She said not a word about Harriet to her father. She promised to settle down, pass exams, make him proud. It was what he needed to hear.

Only when Jim left the table for a moment did she put it bluntly: 'Please, Harriet. It's up to you. You can kill me or you can let me live.' She drew a small brown bottle of pills out of her school bag and gave them a little comical shake. Harriet could hardly breathe. 'I thought you'd be impressed!' she said.

'Well, I—'

'Don't tell Dad, please, he couldn't take the strain. You're not like him. You're strong.'

'I'm just going to pop outside for some fresh air for a moment,' Harriet said. She sat on a low bench next to a deserted bus stop, rusty raindrops falling from the shelter to her head. She pressed her feet into the ground. The wrongness between them that Daisy had pointed out began to haunt her. Is that what I am, a fierce neurotic aping calm?

Daisy wouldn't leave them alone that night. She lurked in a side chair like a mascot of ill will. 'I'm a bit worried about the effect of our being together on Daisy,' Harriet whispered to Jim, setting cups on to a tea tray, in the kitchen. She spoke so gently that he only got every third word or so. She tried again. 'Daisy tells me she is feeling suicidal. That you have been suicidal lately about your wife. She says that neither of you is strong enough to have another person coming in. She's got a bottle of pills in her school bag right now. I don't know what to do or say or even think. She's threatened to take them if you and I go on seeing each other. I can't bear the idea of her being unhappy. That's not what I want.'

'This is absolutely monstrous. I won't give in to it. We mustn't. Harriet, I'm so sorry,' Jim began. 'She's suffering now but she will get used to it in time. I know she will. Deep down she wants me to be happy. She sees how lovely you are. If we're sensitive and respect her feelings, she'll come round in the end, please trust me, we've just got to—' but a knock at the door came and it was Daisy. She was wearing a strange expression and holding an empty glass.

'I thought you'd like to know,' she said, 'I've just taken thirty-four Valium. It won't kill me, I shouldn't think; on the web it says "recovery highly likely". It might even calm me down, but we probably ought to get my stomach pumped.' She held up the empty brown bottle, the corners of her mouth twitching very slightly upward. 'Good for the waistline, I suppose!' she said.

Harriet closed her eyes, then stood up clumsily. 'I'm so sorry,' she told the room in general. She tried auditioning desperate solutions in her mind, but none of them would take. 'I'll go home,' she said, 'and you run her to the hospital. I'll be thinking of you and I'm here if you need me but I think it's time for me to withdr—' But her voice failed slightly as she tried to make the word, and she heard the echo of something entirely hollow inside her and it chilled her and made her harden a little against him.

Jim clung to her tightly. 'I don't want to lose you,' he said. 'I don't know what I'm doing. But I am sure we can work something out that we're all happy with and find a way to continue—'

'It's all right,' Harriet reassured him, letting go. 'I can't stay with her so unhappy. My conscience wouldn't allow it.' She put as much softness in her voice as she could manufacture, rubbing his shoulder with the back of her hand. High politeness could sometimes deter emotional collapse, she dimly remembered, and a good sweet ending seemed fitting after everything that had taken place. She whispered to him, gently, 'But thank you so much for everything,' like a small girl leaving a birthday party. 'Really wonderful.' She went over to Daisy and kissed her strongly on the head. She was an excellent loser. But what she was thinking was, No one's skin will ever fall off for me.

*

It was quarter to six on Monday morning. Success! Seventeen stuffed, beribboned, cellophaned fruit baskets were arrayed in sweet haphazard rows on a low display table in the first-floor playing room. Harriet bickered with herself like an old married couple. 'You should be proud!' she remonstrated. 'I *am* proud!' she sighed, but as she swallowed down her marzipan nausea it rose up again like an escalator, over and over. She opened a window to let out some air. Something wasn't working at all correctly, something was grating hard against her, and before her eyes the exquisitely appointed room, her miniature immaculate universe, the pinks and the golds, the lilacs and crimsons and the twinkling light from the theatrical nineteen-twenties chandeliers, all garlanded with autumn's best fruitfulness, seemed to her a disgusting lie. She stood up. Do you actually think you have the power to alter people's lives when you can't even ...? She left her fruit and cradled a doll in her sticky hand, picked up a tiny frying pan, a scrap of felted wool, a tiny racing-green cake shop delivery van.

It was a failure in this setting to be more than five years old. She kicked a rush-matted chair across the floor, genuinely shocked at her behaviour. This is a bad scene, she thought, in a bad style. Tears steamed against her cheeks. For a second she glimpsed herself as her family saw her: monstrous, grasping, marvellously sinister.

Sometimes she thought Colin could be made more happy with her if she underwent one or two physical procedures. For him, might a surgical solution help? The set of her mouth (he thought it indecent, a whore's mouth), well, she could have it curtailed somehow, nipped or ripped in the bud. Here a gash, there some fine darning. They could make her gaze less knowing, as though it couldn't see through people after all. He'd appreciate that. He might allow himself to be nice to her when she was laced up in a sky-coloured hospital gown, purple and yellow at the eyes like a pansy, clutching a cube of ice to her fat lip, mouth laddered with stitching.

She was angry with herself now. She knew the after-effects of these savage emotional indulgences, you felt them far into the next day as though it were brandy and kegs of ale you had swallowed down, and then everything about you felt indefensible and coarse. Why do you insist on doing it to yourself? she protested. When, she demanded roughly, will you learn?

But I've been good for so long! She hadn't even hinted to the girls that her family loathed her (not that in a million years she would have done); surely there was credit there? She wanted to tell them vaguer things about love and loss and safety and risk and the greater danger of avoiding risk which was a sort of dying. She knew that children were naturally exhilarated when you spoke to them of unsuitable subjects, but that did not make it correct.

Colin would like a compact sister, gap-toothed, uncertain, rose-bud mouth, shoulder-length light hair, demure, dainty-footed, acquiescent. He would choose someone like Flora's mother with her utterly correct physical proportions. She could make her flame-coloured hair mousy brown; Scaredy Mouse – was that the name of the shade he would prefer? Of course a severe trauma might do it naturally, or one of the degenerative illnesses.

She shook herself free of these thoughts. Miss McGee was smiling down at her, mildly impatient, head inclined. This is a man whose idea of high daring, Miss McGee reminded with exquisite timing, is to devour a Scotch egg purchased at a motorway service station, in the back of his car, wiping his mouth with proper shame, and then, breathing heavily, stuffing the greasy wrappings into the glove compartment where they would radiate guilt, for hasty removal later on.

When Isabella and Lucy found themselves in the same maternity ward, they recognised each other instantly from Charterbury, their junior school. Brand-new babies were snoozing in lacy shawls on their wildly reddened chests. They chatted blissfully in whispers.

'Look at her little ear,' Lucy said. 'It is a work of art if I say so myself.'

'I had no idea he would have so much hair,' Isabella marvelled. 'It smells very slightly of malt vinegar.'

'May I compare thee to a summer's chip!'

'Shh!'

'Maybe they will marry.'

'They could both do a lot worse, but of course it's early days.'

'Did you have to have stitches?'

'No. Sorry!'

'It's okay. Someone'll come along in a minute and shove a painkiller up me, I expect. It's insult to injury.'

'I know!'

'Bella, have you had any school thoughts?'

'Well, I went to see a few nurseries but they were pretty grim. There was this one place near me and there were twenty girls sitting in rows colouring in triangles with yellow crayons and squares in green and circles in purple and I just thought what's the point? How about you?'

'Same. I went to Little Oaks – you know, with the fabulous reputation—'

'Supermodel school run—'

'That's it. You have to put the name down before the kid's born pretty much, anyway the three year olds were just writing pages and pages of joined up 'a's, pages and pages of 'b's, pages and pages of 'c's, all sitting in silence. It was like an exam room. Really soul-destroying. I kept thinking, why are they not playing? It was a sunny day, they should have been outside, mucking about. Do you remember that nursery school we went to for a bit before Charterbury?'

'Almost. What was she called again? Margaret?'

'Harriet! How could you forget?'

'Because I was like, four?'

'I remember everything. I remember that big pink room filled with toys. I remember that whatever I said I wanted to do she always said "Absolutely!" I remember when it was Halloween that time she covered the whole place in woolly cobwebs and pom-pom spiders and there were like a thousand pumpkins all flickering, and pink iced buns hanging from the ceiling on strings and we knelt on the floor and tried to eat them wearing black cat costumes. And apple bobbing and then all the parents going "Oh my God! Everything's so amazing." I think I've still got a picture of you and me standing next to a gingerbread house we made there. It's so elaborate. It even has windows. D'you remember? She melted clear mints in a double boiler and left them to cool. I thought if someone is prepared to go to all that trouble on my account, then I can't be *that* bad.'

'She was really inspired.'

'I'll never forget that time I drew all over the piano with green felt tip. I knew I wasn't meant to, and she didn't even tell me off. It was one of those indelible markers as well and some guy came from a piano shop and took half the keys away for a couple of days and brought them back perfect again. And she wasn't even cross. All she said, was, "I shouldn't really have left that pen lying about." I was so moved.'

'I can't quite remember what happened in the end.'

'I just remember seeing her face and thinking that her heart had broken. I remember saying that to my mum.'

'And what did your mother say?'

'She just said, "Don't be so idiotic," or something along those lines.'

'Nice.'

'I know, but you know, with my mum, I don't mean anything nasty by it, but even her biggest fan would say that she's a total sadist. I mean— Oh, hello! I think he's waking up now. Time to open the milk factory.'

A Fraction of a Second

The gasps of pleasure and trills of delight as her parents and children took in the astonishing Harvest Festival display could not be denied. 'I will remember this day for ever, even after I am dead,' Lucy said.

Somebody's courtly grandfather murmured, 'What a tremendous gift you have, my dear.'

'Not at all.' Harriet lowered her eyes.

'It's unbelievable!' Tina pronounced, her mouth hanging open. 'Unbelievable!'

'I'm going to take some photographs for the newsletter,' Linda said.

'You did all that for us,' Flora whispered, gesturing at the branches and foliage hanging from the walls, dressed with garlands of flowers and fruits and birds' nests, feathery peacocks, sugar field mice, heads of sweetcorn.

'This is the best thing ever!' Clementine said.

Even Clementine's evil father was forced to concede a swift 'You have gone to town'.

'Triumph isn't even in it!' Serena judged.

'Must have taken up your whole weekend,' Tina said.

Harriet nodded, smiling. 'Well' – she coloured – 'well ...'

Honey, arriving slightly late, gasped and pointed and clasped her chest and blushed and grinned. 'Three cheers for Harriet!' Honey led the childish cries. 'Hip hip ...'

Perhaps it *was* worth it, Harriet thought with some confusion. Maybe I was wrong to have so many misgivings ... 'And one for luck with a coconut! ...' I don't know anything any more. For a fraction of a second she allowed herself to picture her mother and her brother in the room, gazing rapturously at the deluxe autumnal still life that was her mantelpiece. If they had no reason to suspect that it had anything to do with her, they would vent their admiration, surely?

'Once upon a time,' Honey spoke dreamily, *'there were two little dogs, called Eggs and Bacon. Eggs had a yellow collar and a white lead and Bacon had a red collar and a pink lead. And Eggs had a yellow and white woollen knitted sleeveless fluffy jacket and Bacon had a red and pink woollen knitted sleeveless fluffy jacket and they lived all alone in a big white house with their owner, who was three years old and called Amelia ...'*

Harriet, loose-limbed and soft-shouldered all of a sudden, was so happy to have her girls again that her mood of renewed contentment bordered on exultation. She asked herself smoothly because she liked very much the feel of the thing, 'Are you the only person on the planet who thinks the strains of life are substantially lifted by a roomful of under fives?'

Harriet took the register, surveying the seventeen little faces gazing up at her, blithe and trusting, feminine and serene: Mia, Isabella, Genevieve, Clementine, Cecily, Evie, Katie, Violet, Lily, Flora, Susannah, Miranda, Iris, Clara, Lucy, Alice and Beth.

She made a few rapid mental calculations as to where her

loyalties had taken root. It was not that she had sought favourites, for that would be the most hackneyed way to proceed, feckless, Brodie-ish. Yet the highly strung intelligent girls, the ones to whom she allowed herself, a little, to be drawn, had immediately declared themselves. These were Isabella, Flora and Lucy. Lucy was already slightly chubby and she had noticed and she minded and she had made up her mind to be brave. It was quite touching. Flora was sensitive and emotional. Her caring for any dolls she saw as sick or injured could bring a tear to the eye. Sometimes, when Flora looked at you, there was a sense, only mildly far-fetched to be fair, that she had, at that moment, conceived her first genuine passion.

Isabella had such an intelligent bearing, inclining her head like one to whom deep thoughts came easily. Her conversation was impressive and thoughtful: brilliant with its adult concepts, its 'introduces', its 'apparentlys', its casual 'besides'. She was conscientious, she was anxious; a perfectionist who made of herself, at four years old, the highest of demands. Her maturity was not a poignant thing exactly, for it had a steady base of confidence and resolve. If she was very slightly spinsterish at heart, then, well, it merely gave the school an extra *raison d'être* – the lightening up of her.

Other girls distinguished themselves in a variety of ways: Cecily and Evie were wildly enthusiastic about everything, which was always heartening; Genevieve and Miranda could turn three cartwheels in a row, Clementine liked to retreat into her imagination where enchanted woods flourished and knights and knaves and rouged wicked queens. Mia was very funny, Alice was quite businesslike about everything, Beth could belt a tune, Iris was cuddly, Susannah strong, Katie loved feeding yesterday's noodles to the squawking chickens. Clara was obsessed with numbers, Violet was always daydreaming and Lily loved digging in the garden. These were first impressions but their flavour was powerful.

After school, Harriet retired to her upstairs apartments with a pint mug of tea and a list the same length as her arm. The telephone began to ring. 'Let me just—' She flopped in her father's chair, put the list into her mouth, landed the tea successfully on the lip of the window ledge and with moistened paper adhering to her tongue issued a mangled, 'Herruwallo? Winchester House? May I help you? Hello?'

'I do hope you don't mind a call. My sister said you welcomed family input. She says it's lovely, all pink and white, and that you've got wonderful ideas about everything. I looked up your number on the internet. It looks so gorgeous on the website.'

'Thanks. That's Linda's doing, she's amazing with the – er – who is this please?'

'But she says, she says you're a bit full on.'

'Oh?'

'And, apparently, she's looking for a school, not a belief system, which I think's a bit hoity, don't you?'

Harriet laughed. 'Well, I can be a little . . . ' This is a remarkably odd conversation to be having with a total stranger, she thought.

'Flora Montgomery is my niece. Have you come across her at all or not really?'

'Yes of course. Oh, I see. Hello!'

'Did she tell you that I'm considered strawberry blonde?'

'No, I don't think she mentioned that but we've not talked at length as yet about anything important.'

'I'm in a rather unrefined bin, did they tell you? Well, it's not too bad. The maintenance man is coming round to mend the radiator at eight. It sounds like an excuse for romance – radiators at eight! – but it won't be. I can do candlelight and wine for one – smoke alarms willing – but it's not the same. But life isn't perfection, is it? It's almost perfect though so I mustn't complain.'

'Well, there's no law against it.' This is a remarkably odd conversation to be having with a stranger, Harriet thought again.

'He checks my lottery numbers every week, which is nice. Although I had to have a slight exchange with him. He kept giving me my ticket back with loser written on it. In green ink. Can you imagine? It was too much. There was this raw niggly nerve in me that couldn't take it any more. You don't want loser written on anything, not staring you in the face every single Monday morning. No way to start the week. Of course, I shouldn't take it lying down. I know I could strike back: "You my dear fellow are the loser, and I am one of life's winners, sirrah", but then you're in a slight situation, aren't you? Then he may offer you a drink that you really don't want and the promise of a ploughman's at the weekend when the truth is me and cheese don't get on and then before you know it – trouble. We are not husband and wife. He's actually quite posh. He irons his work jeans.'

'High standards,' said Harriet, smiling broadly at this strange and lovely broadcast. She was beginning to enjoy it now.

'I actually won fourteen pounds on my scratch card last week. I handed it in at the newsagent's and the man said, "You, my friend, are sitting on a goldmine!" Kitty says the lottery is a tax for poor people. She's very joyless sometimes. I don't know why she doesn't manage to wrestle more pleasure out of life. Her life on paper looks so good. I don't understand. Perhaps she plays things down in front of me to be tactful. I loathe tact. Oh, *fuck!*'

'Is everything all right?'

'I can't get these Chinese slippers on. They're a thirty-nine, but everything Chinese is so small, isn't it? Except for their dinners.'

'They can be truly huge, it's true.'

'Can I tell you my plans for tonight?

'Please!'

'Well, it all kicks off with a lemon-oil bath and then I'm going to do a lily and jasmine face mask and have some tea and some lemon shortbread petticoat tails, then slip into said skimpy Chinese slippers *and* the matching kimono – although the kimono's a decent length, you'll be glad to hear, and it covers my bum with a good few inches to spare. Talk soon. Goodbye!'

Harriet blinked and returned distractedly to her limb-length list. As random exchanges went this was certainly— And then she stopped what she was doing and more thoughtfully she pronounced out loud the words 'Well, well, well'.

There was a knock at her door and there stood Serena, confident, mildly equestrian in a refined-looking coat, her perfectly wonky mouth smiling broadly, the dark lustrous hair, the hundreds of pale freckles themselves a reminder that there was humility in this splendid young woman, a sort of urban milkmaid *de luxe* English rose. Yes, Harriet thought with approval.

'Message for you,' Serena said. 'It came through while you were on the other line. It was your mother – she wants you to ring her. It sounded a bit urgent. She left a number. I didn't speak to her – it was on the machine.' She handed Harriet a twist of yellow paper.

'My mother? Are you absolutely sure? She's not phoned me in more than I can't think how long.'

'Er, well that's what she said.'

'And I'm to ring her now do you think? Or should I wait a while? What would be best? Sorry – I don't know why I'm asking you questions you can't possibly answer. It's rather a speciality of mine.'

'Well, she did say to ring right away, but you would know, you know, the best thing ... other people's mothers ... I mean my mother is incredibly impatient so I quite like to keep her waiting, on principle, but then that's just ...' She stopped talking and extracted herself from the room.

Those long stark evenings at home, sitting and hoping her father would telephone some sort of rescue to her from his large important desk, from among the piles of papers, the bone-handled paperknife, the silver-framed photograph of her mother as a startled bride.

The telephone was ringing again. She waited a moment before answering.

'Hello? Winchester House, good afternoon?'

'Oh, hello, dear.' The voice, wary, cheerless, stone and ice, was unmistakable.

'Oh. Hello. How are you, Ma? Lovely to hear from you.' Harriet sat bolt upright, then she stood and kicked off her shoes.

'I'm in London tonight, dear, and I thought we might meet. I'm free for an early supper, or possibly – no, an early supper this evening is all I can offer. But I'm sure you're tied up, it's short notice I know. Perhaps we had best leave it for another time.'

'Great.' Breathe. Slow down. 'That would be really nice.' One two three four. 'Where would suit?'

'I really don't mind,' her mother said.

'Perhaps you'd like to come here and see the school then. Did you hear I've opened a nursery school – I'd love you to see it – and I could make us something delicious or we could go to the place on the corner ...'

'That's good of you but I'm pressed for time ... I've had a long day and as I'm in town anyway I thought we might go to Angelo's.'

Angelo's was the traditional setting for their more excruciating family meals. Angelo himself, eight years ago, belly straining out of his blue and white chef's checks, had shot her such a sympathetic look when she entered his cheerful portals accompanied by her mother, her brother and her sister-in-law that she had wondered if others could see quite how unpromising, on a personal level, they were. It had made the evening almost bearable.

'Fine. What time?'

'Seven. I'll need to be away by quarter to nine, latest. I'll order a car to come at half past eight as I'd hate to get stuck. You just can't rely on black cabs.'

'That'll be lovely,' Harriet said quietly.

'Oh, and Harriet?'

'Hmm?'

'I'm having one or two tests this afternoon. So it's possible I may be a little – I'm feeling awfully weary suddenly. I mean, you may have to ... '

'Of course! But what sort of tests?'

'Please don't be hysterical. I'll tell you about it later, perhaps. Now, is that all right?'

'I'm looking forward to seeing you,' Harriet managed. 'Goodbye.'

Harriet parted her lips to speak, weighing the words in the darkening room. All her mother's offers were bone-dry. 'Why do you not now, nor have you ever been, able to like me?' She put the question in the mildest kindest way into the air. She tried again. 'I do understand,' she would like to console her mother, 'that nobody's perfect, especially me.' But how would she dare? 'I just want things to be ordinary between us. Could you imagine a way I could arrange myself that would make you feel warmly towards me?'

She was determined their meeting would go well. Her mother had not set foot in London for at least a year, as far as she knew. Was there a reason for her calling this meeting now, new information she wished to impart, some sort of change of heart, a softening? What was she being tested for?

It came to her powerfully that what she needed to make this sudden meeting manageable, bearable, recoverable from, and afterwards even mildly laughable, was some bright and blameless new apparel, something in which she might appear beyond reproach. She could choose a new autumn-weight suit of clothes that declared, that had embroidered all over its sleeves, *Don't be alarmed – I have absolutely no axes to grind.* Where did they sell garments like that?

She thought of Flora's mother and how her impeccable clothes mediated the outward signs of her emotional disarray. They set it off beautifully. They distinguished it. Undoubtedly when you looked like that, people would treat you with respect; there would be a minimum of unpleasantness, of waiting and impatience and the ordinary humiliations attached to failure, of people addressing you below your level of intelligence and dignity. She wondered what the charming sister in the 'unrefined bin' was sporting today. It was a mistake to think it did not matter how you dressed in a tragedy.

She caught a bus to the nearest department store, lingered at the entrance where two small boys pushed round and round in the revolving door until one of the security guards came and threatened them with the police. On the first floor she perused the racks of clothes marked *Occasionwear*, evening dresses in the main, in chiffon and silks and silk satin, dark lace, polka-dotted crêpe and bias-cut velvet. In polka dots, her size and strength might be enough to bring on, in an innocent observer, a migraine lasting several days. Where were the defended clothes? Predicament Wear? Disaster Modes? She spied a dress and coat made of the same pinkish beige-coloured wool crêpe. It was exactly the sort of thing she loathed. She lifted it up, she was trying to behave differently after all, but an assistant appeared and advised, 'Hardly anyone can get away with flesh.' Nearby there was a bouclé evening cape which was handsome, which was dignified and distinguished, but it was too outlandish, too thigh-slapping 'principal boy'. On her mother that bobbly wool would grate. She might even think her daughter fancied herself a superhero! Not armour, not chain mail exactly, gas masks, bayonets, she wasn't quite looking for those things. She strode through a skylit atrium of dark and lightish denim, past sportswear and flailing towelling lounge wear, then through lingerie to the boudoir-like shoe studio, then into *Weekend* where she found an ensemble that was quiet, while still retaining notes of gentle cheer.

In the fitting rooms she dressed, Harriet Mansfield, in her brand-new clothes to meet her mother. She would arrive at Angelo's bar and grill quite sedately: the pale spring-weight coat, a green and white drawstring silk blouse with billowing sleeves and a blue-green loosely draped skirt. Librarian mermaid, she thought, flushing, although the skirt could have done with another inch. She opened her bag and rummaged for some tubes and phials and a compact. She would go straight to the restaurant in good time and collect herself before her mother arrived. ('Do alert me when you've got the set,' Jim Rathbone Jones, the man with the daughter, would have said.) She squeezed a coil of light orange make-up into her palm and spread the oily creme across her face, drawing it down an inch or two on to the skin of her neck, smoothing it in over her temples and blending it carefully above her top lip. She looked at herself quizzically in the mirror. If only Serena were here to perform the task with her expert touch. She dabbed some pale powder over the creme to take the orange down a shade or two then added a bit more creme. The resulting complexion had an uneven blobby texture but the colour was uniform in a precise impersonal way. She smeared some forest-green shadow on to her eyelids, an instant mistake, for it was madly brighter on the skin than in the palette. She put a little more of the make-up creme on her nose where the powder had flaked and added a bit more powder for good measure. She sneezed loudly and pinched some colour back into her cheeks, then she drew two straight lines in matt Aristo-Claret on her lips, finally coating her eyelashes quite thickly in brown mascara. Two weary mud-caked centipedes gazed back at her. She shook her head and laughed bitterly at her handiwork. *Never Mind* by Harriet Mansfield, *Awful but Cheerful,* a survivor's guide.

She paid for the clothes on her back and the assistant fished for the tags at her hem and wrists and at her neckline. His touch, cool and fluttery, amused her.

Angelo was a delicate man, sensitive and shy for a restaurateur, and he wore his impressive girth unconfidently, with anxiety, but he liked to please people. His heart went out to his customers in all their various situations and he knew, his food almost said it out loud to you, that a good square meal on a large oval plate, in times of trouble, could be a terrific boon.

Harriet, fifteen minutes early, took a seat at a corner table with a green and white checked cloth. A neat Italian waitress looked after her, bringing her water and bread sticks and olives and caper berries and Italian bread and a little dish of green olive oil and a glass of straw-coloured wine. Harriet opened the collected short stories of an American writer, a suicide, who had once been called 'the bitterest poet in America'. The hero of the story was reading a newspaper on the fourth of July, while waiting for a friend to arrive. All the headlines were terrible. A notorious continental pervert was being feted in New York; a ravishingly beautiful Hollywood star was to undergo a dangerous rectal operation at Mother of Christ Memorial Hospital. Her eyes widened.

At two minutes to seven Harriet braced herself for her mother's arrival. She would stand on seeing her, loosening the table a little and moving to one side the items the waitress had brought so that she could rise without inelegance, without sending furniture or glasses flying across the room. She pictured her mother in a crisp white shirt with the contents of a dish of olive oil splattered across her chest. She bit her lip. At five past seven the waitress brought her a paper and she opened it out, spreading the pages so they housed her. I am the news, she thought. She took a sip of her wine and read a story about childhood obesity. She moved on quickly to an item about domestic violence against pets and finally found a long interview with a TV actress she had never heard of who was discussing in detail her drug addiction. 'And then I phoned social services and asked if they'd take my boy, because I couldn't cope any more, but they refused when I told them my name. They thought it was a publicity stunt.'

Harriet leafed through the television pages. It was seven nineteen. She drained her wine glass and counted all the olives in the dish and the grissini and the slices of bread. A couple walked in, high-spirited, flecked with rain. The man announced to the room that he was starving. 'You're always starving,' the woman said, good-humouredly.

It wasn't at all that Harriet was spoiling for a fight – she would take her mother's delicate post-test state very seriously – but the thoughts were in her head none the less. You could only live your life in character. Don't be afraid, she said. She didn't want her mother to be afraid. It was not her intention to face her with anything – how could that help? – but thoughts were swarming thicker and darker in her mind and the sharp ache had begun again. Harriet shook her head. It was seven thirty-two. It was obvious she wasn't coming. To be stood up by your own mother! The quality of rejection was familiar but there was always something new in being shunned.

Surely it is I who am entitled, after how they have behaved, to shun *them*. To shame them! she protested silently. Why do they refuse to forgive me when I'm the one who has done nothing wrong?

Miss McGee shook her head and at the very corner of her eye there sprang a tear. I was a little child! What could I have done? Some images of violence started up in her, forceful, dreadful, compromising things.

Miss McGee nodded, she was with her, at her side, rooting strenuously for the small girl whose head was being knocked half senseless by her mother against the gaily flowered wallpaper in the nursery. Her brother, almost four years older, watched them in paralysis, hands pasted to his sides. The father, as always, was unfailingly away.

Over the green gingham cloth, with its little satellites of olives and bread and oil and water and wine, Harriet cried out in ugly heaving sobs that sent her arms flailing and her glass and the bread basket and the shallow bowl of oil crashing wildly to the ground. She watched her courage leaving, half mesmerised. She feared

suddenly for everything that pertained to her. She felt her height
and her strong red hair and her large feet to be universally coarse
and menacing. 'If only I could understand why she wanted to, why
she needed to – I know I must have had a part to play ...'

'Listen to me, Harriet.' Miss McGee's voice was sharp with
emphasis. 'You did absolutely nothing to deserve what happened.
You were a little child. You were wholly innocent. Absolutely no
blame belongs to you. It was a travesty of care.'

Harriet was calmer now. Miss McGee's words were shaming to
a certain extent, but there was solidarity there. 'I know I must have
caused it. I must have earned it.'

'Well, that's what we must work on together.' Miss McGee was
almost presidential in her certainty. 'Until you know with every cell
of your being that it just isn't true.'

As quickly as it had begun the little scene was over. Harriet
wiped her face on her sleeve. 'Why do you put yourself through it?'
she asked, but it wasn't brutal, the question, there was compassion
there.

She looked up to see that the restaurant was entirely silent and
both Angelo and the nice waitress were removing items from the
stained tabletop and flapping a fresh cloth across its surface, just as
her girls did when they made up the babies' beds. Beneath them a
waiter set at the floor with a sky-blue towel, picking up the shards
of glass, mopping the oil. Now they were situating new bowls of
olives and bread and everything on the tablecloth again as though
nothing had happened at all. Angelo's palm rested gently on her
shoulder. She regretted immensely the hideous clown make-up.
What must she seem?

'May I sit?' he asked her carefully. He refilled her new glass with
her permission.

'Having a bit of a bad day,' she said. 'Well, some of it was very good, but the last bit . . . But I feel better now. Thank you. I'm terribly sorry,' she finished. 'And she might have tried to get here; she might be ill or something. She was having tests today, so it's possible something wasn't quite . . . They might have kept her in, I suppose . . .'

Angelo gazed at her calmly and warmly for almost a minute, then he parted his lips. 'It's very very hard this life sometimes,' he said. 'All the disappointments and shocking things that come . . .' He took her hand briefly then let it fall. 'I don't know what happens, but God loves you, he blesses and loves you always. You know, he has never left you since you were born, and even before you came into the world he thought of you with such tenderness.' His voice cracked a little, and he dusted a line of flour from his chin and buried his face in his wine.

It was a lovely idea.

Before

Monday

They like us all to keep a diary here for some reason so here goes.

Pa dropped me in the morning. He offered but I said absolutely no need to come in. He was grinding his keys into his palm; there were white marks. He could not be more allergic to this place. I think it made him feel ill even just to drive into the car park. Bad enough for him that I'm here, without him having to witness me trying to make everything all right. He hates feeling embarrassed. He can't bear for things not to be correct. But how can I make this correct? They asked for my belt and shoelaces which was a bit over the top, I mean I know I'm – anyway I'm just glad he didn't have to hear that. I wasn't wearing a belt so that was fine but I wouldn't have worn my brogues if I had known. With no laces my big feet feel like Charlie Chaplin's.

It was outside time very soon after I arrived and we stood in groups in a little courtyard chatting and those who smoked had their cigarettes. It was freezing and my breath was white. I saw his car was still in the car park. I tried to catch his attention but he didn't see and drove away.

Some of the people had blankets from the common room

wrapped around them and looked a bit like refugees. Coffees were brought out on a tray, decaf, and I held one for the warmth, not drinking. My mug said *Wiggins Teape Paper Supplies*. There was a plate of plain biscuits. We clomped about like clowns in our shoes. I am the tallest person here, man or woman, inc. the doctors, and the only person with red hair.

People are friendly. They say, Have you just got here? and How you doing? and things like that. One of the senior nurses Kath who is my care worker offered me a toffee which I said no to, but she said to keep it up my sleeve for a rainy day. She's very nice. She has two grown-up daughters one of whom, Cindy, is a dental hygienist in London, in Harley Street. Her boss is taking the whole practice to Paris for lunch on the Chunnel for their Christmas outing. It's only three hours door to door, apparently it's going to be an eight-course meal!

My room is like a child's room, a bed, a chair, both pink, a roman blind with flowers and birds, all pink, a TV with a little crocheted mat on top, pink, a picture of some shire horses in a white frame and one funny thing, a kidney-shaped dressing table with a little gathered skirt and a three-part hinged mirror as if this was a finishing school! The place seems to be in a U shape. Single bedrooms and bathrooms around the outside then the nurses' station leading on to the lunch area, and the common room in the middle. I like almost everyone here. The food isn't bad. There is a suggestion box if you want something in particular. I have joined the 'pudding club' already and apparently once a week a few of us – not the anorexics – will be in charge of choosing and cooking a pudding. If we make a list of the ingredients by Wednesday morning Kath will buy them for us. This Friday we are going to do Baked Alaska which has four ticks for difficulty in the book! We'll probably need to do two, Kath says, because one won't stretch.

Some people are in just for depression as far as I can tell, although with most people there's drugs as well or alcohol, or not eating. The drugs people all seem very matey. Sometimes they sing We Gotta Get Out of This Place, pretending to be drunk. They say, Can you imagine what it will feel like never to have another drink again in your whole life? One day at a time, the nurses say. There's a rumour that at the edge of the grounds there's a little patch of magic mushrooms. The anorexics have their food in a separate room as their meals sometimes drag on for hours apparently. Some of them look as though they're about to snap, they're so moody and sad-looking, especially their knees and their elbows. Makes me so sad to see them. One of them Sarah caught me looking at her today. I really wanted to help. She said, Why are you looking at me like that I know I'm disgusting. I burst into tears but luckily Kath was around. She's not well, it's her illness talking, Kath said. There are 36 people here, aged 16 to about 80. I am the second youngest. The 16 year old Lily makes absolutely no sense. They put me next to her and we talked for nearly an hour and I had absolutely no idea what she was saying. She is very warm though. Kath implied she might be one of those people who was probably highly strung anyway and then taking Ecstasy pushed her over the edge.

A funny thing my main doctor is called Dr Prince. We met this morning. There are lots of jokes as in Some Day My Prince Will Come etc. etc. as he has a reputation for running late. He is very handsome and dark with a severe-seeming face but actually he smiles and laughs quite a bit. He does have a sad look sometimes.

It is lovely here really. I think more than anything in life I like chatting to people and that's pretty much what we did all day today. Just nonsense, but even still, about television and our feelings and things. Wonder if I could have a chatting job when I leave college! I think it's the least lonely I have ever been. In the common room there is a sandwich toaster and a plate with cheese and ham and tomato slices and two loaves of bread, one white and one brown. In the afternoon they let us watch a video because it was raining. *Singin' in the Rain.* I cried all the way through, feeling stupid, but I wasn't the only one. The 80 year old lady held my hand which was nice. She said she met Debbie Reynolds who plays the main person in Piccadilly Circus once and gave her the wrong directions to the Strand. People here who have been to other places say they were really terrible by comparison with a lot of frightening people, aggressive and violent stuff going on. I am fine in here it's my shitty life outside I can't cope with, a woman called Teresa said. She has a two year old and a four year old who are with her mother in Southend. She has a lot of scars on her arms. There's one man here Robin who told me he thinks all women are cunts, but he has been badly let down in life so you can't really blame him. His wife went off with his brother and then he found out his daughter was sleeping with his best friend. Aren't the men to blame as well? I didn't ask him that. Another lady, Ruth, she is the 80 years one, seems to sing a lot of hymns but I like that. It's relaxing. She has a lovely voice. Her favourite one goes:

> *Walk with me, O my Lord,*
> *Through the darkest night and brightest day.*
> *Be at my side, O Lord,*
> *Hold my hand and guide me on my way.*

It's actually a bit lovely here. I wrote a postcard to Colin saying, Wish you were here, it's got a picture of crossroads on it and some flower beds with marigolds and a set of traffic lights. Sorry about the extremely boring picture on this postcard I put in the PS. I told Kath that he is the person I love most but that he doesn't feel the same way.

She asked me why not.

I don't know. I said that when I was really small he used to let me climb into his bed for a cuddle and he used to tell me wonderful stories about clowns and acrobats and pirates and everything. But then he stopped. I don't know why. Growing up I suppose. He's the only person who really knows me but I frighten him.

Why do you say that? she asked.

I don't know. I don't know. I think I remind him of something. I started to cry and could not stop. Don't know what I'm doing.

College has given me some work to get on with if I am able, but they say I can redo the second year if I want and the LEA will pay my tuition to repeat the year if it's what I decide. Everyone is being so kind. I know I have a lot of making up to do. I really didn't mean to upset anyone. I would never ever do that. I just hope hope hope hope hope I will be able to sleep tonight.

It's not real life in here. We don't really have to be proper people. It's such a relief! Know that sounds pathetic. Is it the first time I can remember ever that I haven't had a headache I am wondering???!!!

I am writing this bit now in the middle of the night. I can't sleep. I say that thing over and over again that Kath told me, I am safe and all is well. I am safe and all is well. Kath is a great believer in talking to yourself nicely when the going gets tough. I mustn't be embarrassed, she says. Tell yourself you're doing well because you are, she says. It's not all bad.

Morning. I just about got through the night. I am having to be very strict with myself when I get bad thoughts. The 80 year old woman Ruth couldn't sleep either so at half past five we got up and

89

crept into the common room and made toasties in our dressing gowns, feeling very daring, one cheese, one cheese and ham. I gave her mine in the end as my stomach couldn't take it so early in the morning. I try to eat but it feels like I'm swallowing sand. She has had a lot of sadness in her life. She had two stillborn babies, well one was stillborn and the other died at two days old – Jessica and Katharine they were called. She showed me photographs of them. They are buried next to each other. She wasn't able to have any more, for some reason. It's odd being a mother to dead children, she said. When people ask her if she has any kids she generally says that she had two girls, but it 'didn't work out'. Her eldest died nearly 45 years ago – there was still rationing. After it happened her mother-in-law – they weren't even close before – said, It's not much consolation but you always will have had them, your daughters. They will always be part of your life in that way, the fact that they were with you for a short while. It helped a little bit, Ruth said. I started to cry then. Her husband makes nativity scenes in walnut shells as a hobby! Ruth doesn't like to be described as a lapsed Catholic because it makes losing your faith sound so casual whereas it was quite traumatic for her as she tells it. She misses her faith very much, but after the girls died she couldn't believe in a God like that. Dave's in a home now, she couldn't manage after he stopped recognising her. He tried to get off with the district nurse one day and that was as much as she could take. Didn't know what he was doing, of course.

He was a good man, she said. When he was still himself.

Are we ourselves? I asked her. She just laughed

On Wednesday if I have been behaving myself, Kath says she can take me into town for an hour's visit. There's a wonderful café there apparently that does cream slices 'to die for'!!!!!

Tuesday

Group therapy today which everyone calls Group, oh so casual! One of the men is Eddy and he traces back his problems to a very possessive mother who got a job first as a cleaner then as a dinner lady in his school because she couldn't face the separation from him every morning. He never knew his father. They slept in the same bed till he was ten and then he made a stand and insisted on his own room. When he left home at 28 she tried to kill herself. He's an only child. She comes to his flat four times a week to tidy up. Pretend I'm just the cleaner you don't have to talk to me she says. He calls her his smother, then feels terribly guilty.

I can't trace my problems back to anything like that. It's just something in me feels wrong. It's not that there's something bad about me exactly, just that lots of things, ordinary things that mean things to other people, don't touch me. I think I have got less feelings than other people, less nerve endings. Something's missing. I know that everything that's gone wrong for me in my life is completely my own fault. I cry a lot, all the time, but I don't feel anything. I talk to Kath about what it would feel like if I did feel things more, what would be good about it and what might be not so good, which is how they express 'bad' round here. I'm not convinced.

Wednesday

Today Kath took me into town. More dramas. Kath says there is always something. It was raining so I wore my mac. She had one too almost the same. Maybe we look like a pair of old spies she said and I started to laugh. The bus stopped right outside the café which was quite grand with white tablecloths and silver spoons. Shall we share one of their famous cream slices? she said. Do you prefer the fresh cream or the crème pâtissière? The fresh cream was like clouds and there was white icing on top of the pastry layers with a feathered pattern in brown. Kath did an icing course once. You pipe thin parallel lines along the length and then drag a skewer very lightly across the lines first from the left and then the right, alternating. It's very effective, she said. I'll teach you if you like. It's relaxing.

Next to us was a terrible couple. The woman was wearing a shocking pink dress with a double strand of pearls. She was about 60, matching pink nail polish. They were having a very late lunch. It's much more expensive than usual, he said, all miserable when the bill arrived.

What you forget is that when you come here with Janet she doesn't drink, so . . . Her voice trailed off sadly.

The cream slice looked delicious and I tried to have a spoonful but I knew I wouldn't be able to keep it down. I started to cry. Kath was very nice about it. Always crying now. I am like a fountain am I not? Kath laughed. Seen worse, she said.

Her daughter is trying for another baby. She wants three girls in total, three backing singers, she says. She has a lovely voice according to Kath.

After tea we decided to take a stroll and look at the cathedral. We crossed the road but from nowhere a bicycle appeared and went straight into me, sent me flying. Kath helped me up. I wasn't hurt it was just the shock really. I was OK, a bit shaky, tiny graze on my forehead, but nothing really but she said I must go to Casualty for an X-ray. As I hadn't really hurt myself I thought it was all a bit over the top. Let's just go back, I said.

No no, she insisted we had to get an X-ray.

I am fine, I protested.

Look, she pointed, we are five minutes' walk away. I'm not talking ambulances and sirens. The X-rays will be clear but if we go back to the clinic they will make us come back to the hospital, it's all to do with the insurance, so we may as well sort it out while we're here. It will be an adventure.

Casualty was quiet at half three on a Wednesday. You have great timing, Kath said. She is so cheery. I don't know what her secret is. Her daughters make her very happy. They said straight away that the doctor would see us but we waited hours, reading ancient magazines. Kath did a quiz on me about whether I was a superwoman or not and then I did it on her.

If your husband came back from work and said, Sorry dear, my boss and four colleagues are coming for dinner in an hour, what would you say? I asked her.

I would say, Where the fuck have you been these past twelve years! Kath roared with laughter. It was quite funny.

We did the X-rays then waited for another hour. Kath phoned the clinic to let them know. The doctor was a young Chinese woman, very softly spoken. I think Kath asked for her specially. Kath came in with me. She asked us to sit down. I've been looking at your X-rays, she said.

I'm completely fine. I only came because she insisted. I don't want to waste anybody's time, I said.

Well – good to be careful, the woman said. She studied my X-rays which were clipped to a large illuminated screen. They looked all ghostly, the navy regions of my brain, the white bone, the cloudy, unclear areas, the blank bits, the sockets and the shadows. I was embarrassed. It was almost worse than being naked!

Tell me about your history of head injuries, she said to me.

Don't have one.

It's clear from your X-rays that your head has suffered a series of blows. Have you been in car accidents in the past? Or did you play a lot of contact sports at school?

I don't know what you're talking about, I said.

The woman looked at me strangely. No?

You sure that's my head you've got up there?

The woman tapped with a ruler at the areas of concern on the photograph. You see here and here, there's evidence of a number of contusions to the lobes, here at the back mainly. It may well have been from when you were a child, before the bone was fully formed, as there is a certain amount of denting, here – she pointed at different bits on the picture, and then started asking me all these questions like, When you were a child was there a serious fall at home? Or horse riding? Or was there a problem with . . . ?

I looked straight into the doctor's face which was bright white suddenly. I don't mean to pry, she said. I just want things to be clear. She added, It's just routine. The doctor tried with me again. Do you suffer from bad headaches may I ask? I didn't answer but Kath said, She has told us that she has had a headache her entire life. You don't mind me saying that, do you, pet? It's just important that the doc has the full picture.

That's OK, I think I said.

I shut my eyes. I thought maybe I was a bit concussed after all. I couldn't think of anything. The doctor came over and took my hand, but I didn't want her to touch me, poor thing, so I pushed her away and then I felt completely hopeless with tears all over me and my head just drooped and there was wet all down the front of my shirt and I took my head in my hands and crossed my arms over the top of it and sank deep into the chair and then I was howling wildly and uncontrollably, choking sobs, I couldn't believe those loud sounds were coming out of me, all those shrieks and cries beating hard against the walls of the room and it was completely stuffy and claustrophobic and boiling hot suddenly.

I remembered we were playing Ludo in the kitchen, one time, something we did a lot, me and my mother, and the phone rang and it wasn't anything important but we had this telephone pad in the hall and it had this little silver pen attached to it in a little narrow side pocket and she couldn't find it and she got so upset she just came after me.

Of course you can't remember pain exactly, but you remember the shame of it and the horror and also why was she doing this? Did she think I had taken the silver pen? I never ever took her stuff, in fact I always checked the pen was there when I got back from school. But there was so much horror in her face and and all the while I had the feeling that she was horrified too, but the noise of my head going into the kitchen wall again and again and then against the sharp door frame and all along the wall of the hall with clumps of hair flying on to the floor or muddled up inside my clothes, in my buttonholes and ripping in my zips. And the next thing I was crying out in these ugly agonising sobs and my head was jerking about trying to find a space in the air where there was comfort or welcome or safety and then it was impossible suddenly to breathe and I gasped for air but there just wasn't any and my head went crazy with the most terrible aches and screams flew out of me and it was all entirely against my will, because I am not a brash person, I'm only 18 and I know I'm nothing and not for all the world do I want anyone to think that I'm attention-seeking.

Kath came and stood behind me with a hand resting gently on my shoulder. She was brilliant really. The doctor sat with us in silence, and no one said anything for a long time and then the sun went down and in the end I stood up and Kath and the doctor talked about me in the growing darkness.

I want you both to come and see me again next week, the doctor said, and together we'll make, and she said the word so grandly, as though it could solve everything, a plan.

Thursday

Well, the doctors at the clinic are mad for me after yesterday's little episode. I am suddenly a superstar. I have made progress in a very interesting way, they feel. They were very interested in the 'mechanism' of my repression, they think that my memory must have just shut down for me about all this, fenced it off from me, and they think it's 'terrific' that my memory is up to being straight with me. Not completely sure about that.

Kath got cross. You need to be a little bit more sympathetic and a little bit less fascinated, she said to them.

I'm sorry about all this, she said. You know what people are like, she said.

With your permission we shall invite your mother to the hospital they said and challenge her.

No. I put my foot down. I kept it down. She doesn't deserve that, I said. They got so cross but I wouldn't back down.

I put my foot down about Ma, but they insisted so to get them off my back I said you can invite my father if you really have to. So Pa came back today. I knew it wasn't going to be water off a duck's back to him. He wore a suit and a tie as I think he came straight from the bank. I hate the idea of him missing work because he loves it there.

I am not good at this kind of thing, he said when the doctor thanked him for coming. I couldn't help feeling proud of how perfect he looked. Even Prince looked like a scruffbag next to him and he was in a pinstriped suit and a bow tie!

Kath promised me she would be nice to him and so she started trying to make him feel better. You don't have to be good at being here, it is just great that you were able to come at such short notice, Kath said, or something like that, trying to be kind.

Thank you, he said. He sat stern and terrified, in his jacket and tie, like someone regal from Edwardian times. No one had even said anything yet but already it was torture for him.

I could hear him breathing uncomfortably and I had never heard that before. He poured himself a glass of water and drank it and poured another one and then another one.

I thought I had better get things over with before he drowns himself. I am making progress, Pa, I said. I am trying my best. I am grateful to be here. I know it's much nicer than other places of this ilk.

Ilk, is that a word? Doesn't sound like one. (I am too ashamed to write down here what it costs here a day. I will pay them back one day.)

Thank you, Harriet, he said, which I thought was odd.

I am trying to understand certain things about our family. Nothing makes sense, I said.

He nodded his head which seemed encouraging but then he nodded for the next minute by which time it seemed more like a nervous tic.

I don't know what to say to you, Harriet, apart from the fact that we have all made terrible mistakes about which we are deeply sorry and ashamed.

I am sorry too, Dad. I really am.

He kept shaking his head and crumpling and smoothing and stretching out a big white handkerchief in his hands. All I can hope is that I have been a better father to you than my father was to me and you will be better than I was with your children and they will be better than you and their children will be better than their parents and on and on and on . . . and things will I hope get happier in that way.

It's a good idea, I said.

Are you aware that when Harriet was a small child, repeatedly and systematically – we think it may have stopped when her brother was sent to boarding school – Harriet's mother was in the habit of— Prince began. But I stood up and shouted over his voice. He was very taken aback.

You promised I would be in charge of what was said. You cannot break a promise like that.

My father shook visibly in his chair. I felt for him so much sitting there. Poor thing. What was he meant to do? What was he meant to think? He hated raised voices, let alone— Can you die of embarrassment? I wanted to hold his hand. He didn't deserve this.

Kath took my side: She is right. You cannot promise one thing and do another, she said. It is not acceptable practice. While we all were ganging up on Prince Pa suddenly said, I apologise unreservedly for my part in everything. And then after three minutes of utter silence, Grave mistakes have been made. And two minutes later, Would it be monstrous of me now if I headed back to town?

I stood up and for a terrible moment I thought he was going to shake my hand, but he reeled me into him, for a very sharp embrace, and then he spun me away again.

We will be in touch, the doctors said.

Thank you, he said, with so much relief that I thought he might sprout wings and fly out of the door.

Well, that was a wasted opportunity, Prince was saying.

I don't think so, I said.

I just didn't want you to be cheated out of what was yours, Prince said.

I started to cry then. Someone give her some tissues, he said with irritation. I was grating on him I could tell, but I did feel a funny kind of – triumph, was it? He had been intimidated by my father and the feeling had caused him embarrassment. Ha!

Well done, Kath said.

Friday

Prince wanted to talk endlessly about Pa's visit. Humour him, Kath said. He's a bit of a wally sometimes but he is a good man and he's only trying to do his job.

I wonder why you were so eager to let him off the hook? Prince said.

I wonder why you are so keen to nail him to the cross? I said or something similar.

Prince was stimulated by what he considered my 'fighting talk'. He was fingering the corners of his blue bow tie. I think it would be good if you could express some anger, he said.

With you?

Well it would be a start.

I think it would be good if you nipped your bow tie habit in the bud.

He patted my hand. Good girl, he said.

After lunch Prince called an extra therapy session with me and after a while he dragged a chair into the middle of the room. He was wearing his blue bow tie again and a light yellow shirt. Is he turning into Mickey Mouse?

Imagine your mother is sitting in that chair. What would you like to say to her?

Um. Nothing really. I know that's the wrong answer, but . . .

There aren't any wrong answers exactly . . . Would you like to know what I would say to her?

Not really.

Why are you being so stubborn?

This doesn't feel right.

Ah, he said. Going too fast. It's a fault of mine.

Then I started crying and I just could not stop. I used all Prince's tissues and he went and got another box. Poor man. After half an hour he got Kath to come and sit with me. I don't know what I'm doing.

I don't have to make Baked Alaska tonight, do I? I asked. Kath just laughed. No, darling.

Saturday

I seem to have taken up smoking. It breaks up the day and all the people who smoke here are the nicest anyway. They are always chatting as they puff away. They are changing me on to a newish drug that's very popular in America. When you look at the possible side effects on the box it says loss of appetite, depression and suicide! You could not make it up. Prince wrote 'witty and masochistic' on my notes today. I can't stop crying. I can't sleep. I'm not sure what to hope for. Kath says I have had a big shock and I am doing my best to process it but it's all a bit too much.

I don't think I can take any more.

They have put me on Obs 1 which means one of the nurses has to sleep in my room because I am considered high risk. I wish it was Kath, but she has to go home for her daughter's birthday weekend. If I go down to Obs 2 then the nurse just sits outside my door on a chair and comes in every 15 minutes. On Obs 3 she comes in every half an hour. Some people from college sent me get well cards which was nice. Kath says the strain of keeping the memory secret from myself could have caused my depression and suicidal feelings. Kath says this stuff coming out could be a real turning point in my life for me. Everyone is being lovely.

Sunday

I have decided I am not going to speak or see anyone in this place again apart from Kath.

Monday

I am not going to eat or drink anything unless they let Kath come to see me. Where is Kath?

Tuesday

You are not yourself, everyone keeps saying. You've had a bad shock. These feelings will pass. I am sleeping a lot of the time now. I like my bed. I say the thing that Kath taught me over and over again. I am safe and all is well. They have put me on different pills again. They are looking after me. My bed is pink with flowers. I am doing all the right things.

Morning After

The next morning broke, painfully shy, the darkness stretching until after Harriet dressed when filaments of sun switched on the sky. In the mirror by the mottled basin Harriet looked remarkably well. The pallor that came from being wronged was flattering, she supposed. That was a first. It lent a bit of triumph to her features, possibly. Only you look too earnest, too deliberately sincere, she judged, like a poet whose poetry was just too poetical and therefore, well, dodgy.

She wished she knew for certain how much of her character her family had invented. A great deal, she hoped, but you were never really sure. You must try to keep a lightness about you, she urged, not the full force of farce, necessarily, but a touch of comedy, like, like, I don't know, like grapefruit spoons.

Her mood dropped, far from comic, the good humour vanishing abruptly. She allowed herself some skewed thoughts: a stab of longing, shaky ground. To be attacked, she supposed, was recognition of sorts, for it was proof you were unignorable. You were to be reckoned with, taken seriously. To be intolerable to another implied a great deal of relationship, she supposed. Neglect, she feared, was the worst kind of annihilation.

And is a bollard distinguished when struck by a passing car? she countered with scorn. Well, I'm not sure, I'm just not sure. At least, at least then it comes into the story.

Come on now, she smiled, as to a child too obsessed with its sweeties. She would treat herself handsomely today. *Treat Yourself Handsomely Today!* by Harriet Mansfield. There was still no word from her mother since she had failed to materialise the night before. You are your own mother now, she self-consoled. It was hardly news.

She hadn't learned much in life, she sometimes thought, but she knew it was important to be civil to yourself. Some of the children in the hospital where she used to volunteer talked to themselves like their most ardent admirers. 'I'm brilliant today,' they would beam, through tubes and drips and wires, their high spirits assaulting the waves of pain.

At nine o'clock, when she drew back the front door, she was needed immediately, essential, in demand. Lucy stood bellowing on the gleaming black and white tiles. Her cheery nanny, with the bright corkscrew curls, picked her up and held her tightly. She was not one of those carers whose compassion dissolved into threats after a minute or two.

Two or three other little girls began to wail in sympathy, in rivalry. 'What's wrong?' 'Has she fallen?' 'Poor little lamb!' the nannies chorused with concern. Harriet descended the front steps rapidly and took one of Lucy's hands. Now three more of the children were sobbing bitterly. The dim street throbbed with miniature distress. It was so terrible it was almost funny. They were drawing stares of horror from passers-by. 'What have you *done* to them?' you almost heard the people cry. 'Nothing, nothing much!' she wanted to respond. There was a tumultuous air, but to an experienced ear she hoped it was exaggerated, teacup-ish. One of the wailing tots was now referring loudly to the time she cut her finger slightly nine months before.

Some of the mothers carried on talking, sharply, unmoved by the screaming girls. 'When I think how hard it is to persuade Thomas to do his homework I marvel at how the Victorians ever managed to get their children up the chimneys . . . ' one mused.

On Lucy's nanny Tessa's mouth there was the distinct thrill of outrage. Her hands were trembling, her silver bangles a small hysterical percussion section. 'You are not going to believe this,' she said, her words heavy with the drama of it, her voice slowed and lowered for maximum intimacy, and there was a dollop of relish there too, perhaps. 'She's . . . she has only gone and cancelled Lucy's birthday!'

There followed loud gasps of awe and disbelief from the gathered mothers and carers.

'Yeah, her mum, as a punishment, just decided that Lucy's birthday, today, no longer exists. Cancelled.'

'But this is monstrous!' Harriet murmured.

'I had to do a ring-round, tell everyone the party's off this afternoon. And I had to tell Lucy as well.'

'No! Let me be clear. They are stopping the party because she did something that she—'

'It's not just the party. It's everything. Today is now going to be an ordinary day. No presents. No special breakfast. No party. All the cards in the bin. No clown. No cake. No nothing.'

'Christ!'

'Lucy was a bit wild and her mother warned her and she was wild again and her mother said, "Right. If that's your attitude I'm cancelling your birthday."'

'"If that's your attitude"? What a ludicrous thing to say.'

The nanny nodded and gave a bitter laugh. Couldn't have been more than nineteen. 'Tell me about it.'

'But she won't go through with it, surely?'

'She's very big on follow-through. She made me phone everyone. Tell everyone the party's off this afternoon. I felt so evil. She phoned the bakery and cancelled the cake. Obviously she'll still have to pay for it, but "Tell them to bin it!" she said. What a waste! And now I've got to take all the presents to the charity shop. She told me to get an itemised receipt because she thought I couldn't be trusted. And Lucy's meant to come with me when I go to learn that "every action has a reaction".'

'This is obscene. And it isn't even true anyway. Many actions go completely unnoticed.'

'I'm not even allowed to give her something myself. I knitted her a scarf and mittens. I can keep them till Christmas, obviously. You can see how upset Lucy is.'

'It's complete sadism.'

'I don't know what to do.' The nanny bent and kissed Lucy's head with such tenderness.

'Give me a moment to think, will you?' A smile spread on Harriet's lips, thoughtful, *de luxe*. 'Leave it with me. I have an idea.'

'Thank you. Thank you.' Tessa was practically curtseying before her, relief brimming from her every pore. 'I just *knew* you'd know what to do. Didn't I say?' she said to her charge.

Coming down on children like a ton of bricks at the first sign of the merest bit of spirit . . . insisting on the strictest of regimes, systems fraught with banal commands and rules and lists of infractions as long as your arm and twisted penalties, fetishised, mean-spirited punishments, all in the name of . . . of what exactly? Cancelling a birthday! It was practically a human rights abuse. 'I cannot tolerate it. I will not tolerate it,' Harriet said.

Well, she would not let Lucy's birthday go uncelebrated. They would make a splendid party at school. All the class would dress up. She would reclaim the cancelled cake, dress the assistants as clowns, set up the Punch and Judy. There would be musical bumps and maypole dancing in the garden, apple bobbing, the blindfolded eating of iced buns on strings.

But I'm not mischief making! Harriet protested playfully to the conjured profile of Miss McGee. I'm correcting an injustice! She's one of my favourite pupils! It's simple restoration. Any human person would do the same! You know *you* would. Miss McGee inclined her head, thoughtfully, but she would not give anything away.

Harriet, during all those years, had understood something of Miss McGee's keen mental processes: her attempts not to say things, her caution, her ultimate appropriateness almost fizzing in the temporary appearance of extra lines on her face. Stress lines, lines of containment. Their meetings had never taken place on an antiseptic stage. As a therapist you would always wish to drop remarks that more properly belonged to a friendship and you had to be strict about it. 'Please tell me you are joking, surely?' 'You absolute dark horse!' 'I am sorrier about this than I know how to say.' 'Over my dead body!' 'You let him have it? Hooray!' This was the sort of thing Harriet observed being pressed away into the corners of Miss McGee's mouth which were surprisingly emotional when you looked closely. It was where she stored her best things. The lips were both long and thin and because of this the mouth was only half full in appearance, but they were intelligent lips. It was an original sort of mouth. Its colour was good. Either

Miss McGee applied a lipstick that was exactly the same colour as her lips, or her lips were soft and well conditioned and even in tone.

The sound of the telephone disturbed her. Her mother apologising at the end of the line! 'I'm so so sorry to have let you down. Do say you forgive me?' Please can it be that, she murmured. She took a deep breath and softened herself to answer. 'Listen, please don't give it another thought,' she would say to her mother with warmth. Sometimes she genuinely couldn't remember what it was her mother was supposed to have done. 'Winchester House?' But the words came out so quietly she had to say it again and the second time it came out harder, rougher, despite her intent. 'Hello? Winchester House?'

'What's up with you?'

'Ah – who is this, please?'

'It is the artist formerly known as Flora's aunt Sophie!'

'Hello there! How are things?'

'Well. There's a bit of exciting news. Can I tell you about my latest glamour purchase?'

'Please!'

'I've got a new winter-weight fluffy cherry-red tracksuit top with burglar proof pockets. Zip-up.'

'Wonderful! Sounds almost Christmassy.'

'I was reading this book, *Avoiding Stress*, it's by an internationally renowned psychologist. There's a chapter called "False Friends". I thought he meant people like Brian the porter who's always nicking fags but he means caffeine and alcohol. Biscuits even. God. Sometimes I wish I could just put up a sign saying Sorry I'm not on speaking terms with the world.'

'Nil by mouth?'

'Exactly.'

'I know what you mean.'

'Of course you do. They want to put me under the smoking clinic, but I'm not keen. I phoned up the Samaritans but they were very short with me because I was on such good form. Can you believe it? How are you doing anyway? Have you been snowed under sharpening the plimsolls?'

'Not quite. Bit of a taxing day. Run-in with a parent. Nothing much. Just one of those things.'

'With my sister?'

'No, no. Not with her.'

'What happened?'

'Obviously I can't go into details; probably a storm in a teacup anyhow. I think I handled it quite ... Sophie? Are you still there?' All was dead at the other end of the line. 'Hello? Can you—' Harriet winced. She thought of the girl, brave and wretched in the psychiatric ward. 'I'm so sorry,' she said into the gathering evening air. She rummaged in her desk and found a postcard of bluebirds. *Dear Sophie*, she wrote.

She tried to think what she would have liked to receive on a postcard when she was at her worst. If someone had drawn for her a map of this school, the coat pegs in the hallway with the embroidered names beneath, the fruit and fabric arranged on a plinth in the art room, the chickens in the garden, it would have dazzled her. It was so much more than an impossible mad dream. Even a simple photo from the future of herself sitting in a café with a coffee and a paperback – not necessarily a fancy patisserie but just a cracked table in the grimiest backstreet hole – would have represented a wonderful leap, and been quite enough to keep her going, if the picture was solid, if the person in the picture was ...

Much of her thirties had been spent in hospitals as a children's visitor. It was kill or cure. She wanted her days to be majestic, but all she felt was nauseous grey. Somebody help me, she sometimes said out loud at night, but no one ever heard. She needed a different setting; contrasts, challenges. She wanted welcomes, but all the people she held most dear were made of wood and stone. It was on one awful Friday, murky and dispiriting, that she had arrived for her first morning. The lady on the telephone, the smiling one who'd organised the training, said to arrive at ten o'clock. She strode up the bald hospital steps, braced for geriatrics, for post-operative waxed-faced jitterers or other assorted health failures. She wasn't squeamish about horrors. She liked to talk. Drips, ill-aligned hips, stitches, wires, scars, twitches – she didn't mind any of that, not at all, why should she? Piss and pus and shit and vomit she was fine with. Perfectly natural. Cries for help, she understood, needed acute hearing. Invalids compelled to flash their wounds and scars, like baby pictures, in the hope of admiration? She would give it to them happily. It was, she knew, considered fitting work for a shaky soul.

She was not a bad person, and for the women or the men lying prone with cellular cotton bedclothes pulled to their necks and cracked plastic beakers on their nightstands, purplish drums of bright wrapped chocolates, sticky grapes, isotonic children's drinks, red and white I LOVE YOU teddies, crumpled *Celebrity Sweat Patch* magazines, things could certainly be a lot worse than . . . than her. She was naturally interested in people, that she would not have to contrive, and if they did not like her, well, what could they do? Physically manhandle her off the premises (Let me go! Let me go! Let me go!) or just an ordinary departure under the usual shadows and clouds?

It was a doomed project from the start, Harriet knew, embarked upon foolishly to prove something to people who had no knowledge of her antics and no interest in anything she did. It was more than no interest, if you faced it squarely – it was complete aversion. Harriet walked along the hospital's fiercely lit corridors towards the assembly point to which she had been directed. The sadness inside her was a searing acid with its own toxicity. She inhaled the reek of exterminated germs as she marched along infinite cheerless passages, her footsteps echoing. She glimpsed wards as she walked, doctors in bleached coats, the pitted bottom of an elderly man hanging sadly from a loosely laced gown with blue squares, a nurse rubbing hibiscus liquid soap into her hands, a man and woman doing a convincing brother-sister act at a relative's bedside. There were large random intersecting segments of colour in the polished lino, sea-blue, lemon, turquoise, all down the hall. It was like a Venn diagram that had suffered a nervous breakdown.

When she reported for duty she was close to tears. She felt the shame prickle on her skin: they wanted robust souls, cheery and convivial, not a whole new intake of self-serving invalids.

Penny, the visitor coordinator, came out to meet her. She smiled so sweetly Harriet was stunned. 'Follow me,' she said. 'I'm glad you're wearing red, it's nice for the children to have cheery colours. I thought I'd try you in the children's ward. Is that okay for you? I did ask Sandra to ring and check, but she's . . .'

'Oh no, that's great. Of course I don't really know if I'll be what they—'

'Oh, don't worry about that. You'll be fine.'

The children's ward was a riot of faded jungle murals. She was instantly out of her depth, but a child approached her, a healthy-looking girl of athletic build with red cheeks and rose-gold hair who smiled mischievously. Then, because something had evidently succeeded, she slipped her hand into Harriet's. The sun beamed generously through the high ward windows. 'Play with me?' she said.

'Yes please!'

It had been months or years since her life had known such triumph. But what if the child began to distrust her affections? They played, twinned, an elaborate game of maritime adventures, with pirates, perilous storms, crashing seas that threatened and soothed by turn, life rafts, charts to check, frazzled cabin-life, sail sewing, bilge pumping, plank walking, tinned bully beef, treasure troves and limes to ward off the dratted scurvy. Other children joined them, a boy with a leg in plaster – 'Arrrgh!' – a boy who was having his large ears pinned back that afternoon. 'Arrrgh!' They were the most beautiful ears that Harriet had ever seen, but the child was bullied mercilessly at school, and she did understand. The teachers, apparently, were beasts.

Then two beds and a table became lifeboats and a dinghy and pillows were lumpy sacks of grain and now there were eight or nine children, one so frail he could barely sit in a chair but insisted on a part to play. Harriet blinked for a moment at the scene of the rolling ocean and the sailors and the two little blonde mermaids who were cooing at them from a distant promontory and through her success a clear picture of bliss appeared in her mind and it was of four sleepers, two large, two small, lying in bed, close together, hand in hand in hand in hand, all through the night.

Well, she returned to the hospital as often as she was able. She was working four days a week at the time, as an office manager in a large Georgian house that had been subdivided into business suites on short-term lets. It was a reasonable job for a reasonable person and she knew she was lucky to have it. That was a difficult time, a few months after her family crash when her brother had commanded her to exit his life. Her routine was bad, that was certain, but she did not know how to turn it round. She woke each morning and flinched as she took the familiar sharp ambush of hurts, trying to close down on them, resolving to be stoical, and all this before she had even opened her eyes. Then on to Miss McGee. Well, it was different now. It was another world. She woke thinking of the children, anticipating their brave delights which when looked at closely were also her own. The irony was not lost on her. She had made Stay Out of Hospital the maxim of her adult life and look where she was now!

She spent the remaining three days of the week with the children. It was as though her heart and her mind were being operated by an entirely different set of strings. The children adored her. She was the gentlest of giants. From her high vantage point they loved the view. They even thought her huge feet had their own mad charm!

At two o'clock Lucy's birthday cake, in the fashion of a kidney-shaped swimming pool, lay in crumbly ruins on its scalloped silver board. Aquamarine icing crusted the cheeks and chins of seventeen exhausted girls. Harriet took Lucy upstairs to see her gifts, bought back quickly from the charity shop, explaining they would have to live at school for now: the bicycle with the wicker basket, the ladybird print swimsuit, the yellow poncho with the kitten motif and the doll in nun's attire. A nun doll? Harriet had wondered . . .

At the sight of the presents Lucy's eyes filled with tears. 'I thought I wasn't having my party! I lost my party but I got it back!' She threw herself into Harriet.

Then it was time for Harriet to climb inside the candy-striped Punch and Judy stand and in the dark heat, her head under the thick black curtain, she helped Punch and his wife reconcile their differences. At the end all was harmony, the cast of characters reunited by their mutual love of sausages. Judy was particularly triumphant. Harriet was dripping sweat, her wrists aching. When she poked her head up above the platform, to take her bow, Lucy was sleeping in a small contented coil.

She was still sleeping when her mother came to fetch her. It was the first time since the start of term that Candida Meyer had set foot in the school. The mother paused for a moment and took in the half-eaten jellies studded with raspberries and the gingham bunting, the striped puppet booth, the discarded pass-the-parcel paper scraps, the ruins of the cake that she had ordered and paid for, with the HAPPY BIRTHDAY LUCY life-saving ring at the rim of the pool. The nanny at her side looked delightedly at the scene, composed her features, glanced at the mother, received an unmistakably withering glance and then a flurried stage direction which commanded her to pick up Lucy and remove her from the room. The mother, pale as flour now, even her eyes, turned to Harriet in unleashed fury.

'Uh-oh,' Honey mouthed at her employer's frank head, taking her bottom lip in her teeth. Linda – squeamish – covered her eyes for a moment, winced, and scuttled back to the downstairs office.

'You,' she spluttered, 'you . . .' Then she fell silent.

She is going to say something entirely hammy, Harriet thought, bracing herself. It was important to keep the power. She gave a derisory glance at the mother's costume, the extremely tight skirt through whose papery fabric the lines of her underwear were clearly visible even from the front; she took in the high, gleaming wine-coloured Spanish boots, the hopelessly *de luxe* peasant shirt, the little fitted jacket made of streaked animal pelts and the snake-skin clutch bag with gilt trim. Harriet stared hard at the delicate pavé diamond necklace on a rose gold chain that bore a short word in very lacy, almost indecipherable italic script: *Cunt.* These people!

Harriet decided to put her case first. She spoke in the very calmest tones she had ever mustered.

'Good afternoon.' She beamed her widest grin. It was a brand of hospitality designed to stun. 'As you see, we always celebrate the girls' birthdays at school. We've had such a lovely time. If you desired me not to make a party, I'm certain you would have given due notification. You might have mentioned it on the admission form in the special requests section, next to the dietary require-ments, did you not see there was a little box?' Slow your voice down, she told herself. 'You might have communicated your wishes to me through the proper channels. When I don't hear from par-ents, when I never ever see them here, I can only really presume that they don't particularly – what's the word – care.'

The mother's eyes, bulging with ill will, saw the bicycle, the nun doll, the swimsuit that was almost sarcastic now with ladybirds, and the heat of her fury substantially increased the temperature of the room.

'Of course, I know nothing about your domestic arrangements,' Harriet added, as if the whole thing were almost more squalid than the teeth and tongue in her mouth could bear.

Ms Meyer looked at the window and tried for composure, breathing heavily, her hand terrorising the innocent fronds of her scarf. Her dilemmas were fraught on her features, fraught in her hands' indisciplined vibrations, fraught even in the wispy strands of her rich chestnut-coloured fringe. You could scream at your employees, at your family, at strangers, at waiters and cloakroom attendants, junior hairdressers, bank workers and lawyers' secretaries (although not at lawyers or high-up hair people), but could you meet with full, fluent asperity the director of your child's school? Not knowing where the power lay did not suit her at all and this fuelled her anger all the more. She was contemplating a shocking act. She lunged forwards suddenly and for a gorgeous moment Harriet thought the mother would strike her, but she spared them both that calamity.

Her voice when it came was surprisingly small. 'Lucy has been behaving disgracefully lately. We decided that she was not going to celebrate her birthday because we had to teach her to do what she was told.'

Harriet, wildly emboldened, decided on this occasion to hold nothing back. She countered sweetly, 'Thing is, I absolutely won't tolerate words like disgracefully used on my premises about four-year-old girls. It's from a register I despise.'

The mother's eyes widened terribly. She took a deep breath that rendered her, for a half-second, oddly vulnerable; like a hollow tree trunk, empty and rootless, she swayed lightly and it was awfully tempting to push her down. 'Last weekend,' her voice looped and surged with anger, 'when I was walking to the park with her after school, Lucy . . . '

Who can be bothered to hear this idiotic rant, Harriet thought. Whatever Lucy may or may not have done has been utterly dwarfed by your conduct, which is monstrous.

Candida Meyer was still talking. ' . . . so she slipped her hand out of . . . ran straight into the . . . '

'Tra la la, fingers in my ears!' Harriet almost sang.

'It's quite a busy road and she was almost hit by a . . . It was the worst moment of my entire ... I talked to her about the dangers when we got home ... she promised it would—'

'So sorry to interrupt! What must you think of us? Honey, would you mind awfully getting Ms Meyer a cup of tea?'

'After that I didn't take her out of the ... I was too shaken ... she doesn't seem to do it with Tessa.'

'Serena! From the petty cash, could you please, we must reimburse Ms Meyer for the birthday cake, it was *so* good – oh, put sundries or miscellaneous or something of that order, I don't know, *trifles*, on the form, perhaps – sorry, do go on ...'

'... time a cyclist almost hit ... I had to buy him a new bicycle. Which was fine ... she could have no television for a week and no cakes or ... Then I said to her if she ever did it again—'

Serena emerged with two cups of tea on a tray and some Marie biscuits. 'Thank you, Serena. Please,' Harriet said and handed Lucy's mother a cup. 'Sugar?' she enquired, mischievously.

'No, I do not want sugar,' the woman hissed.

'The funny thing is that one of our topics for next week is road safety, but I'll start it tomorrow.' Harriet spoke quietly.

'I'm not sure Lucy will be here tomorrow.'

'I'm sorry you feel the way you do.' Harriet stood up. 'It is, of course, your choice.' She stared again at the woman's necklace to see if it really could be believed. Was it some sort of identity pendant? 'Shall we say goodbye?' Harriet made an exit, a haughty, dignified one designed to make the mother feel idiotic.

It was not the behaviour of these women so much as their vocabulary, she thought, with a shiver of pleasure, as she brushed her teeth that night. Her spirits were at least as high as the ceiling and she lowered herself into the hottest bath she could bear. She soaped herself enthusiastically, spreading her scarlet limbs with a shell of creamy foam. There was the throb of pleasure ringing in her head, as though she had just received excellent news.

In her fridge was a bottle of champagne which a parent had given her as a thank you after a rather jolly advice session. Without having given herself permission she hopped out of the bath, raced across the room, retrieved the bottle and a glass and capered back into the bath to open it. She eased off the cork and filled her glass to the brim. She clinked the stem, in a toast, against the lip of the white enamel. The icy bubbles hit the back of her throat and she stretched out in the water, her body suddenly immensely pleasing to her.

The telephone rang and she leapt to answer it. It sounds like Sophie's ring, she thought, large wet footprints, dripping in a towel, adjusting herself for one of their strange merry exchanges. Colin! His voice, scratchy, telegrammatic, ill-aligned.

'Bad news, I'm afraid. Ma's in hospital, terrible pains. We're in France. They think it might be pancreatitis, or,' his voice cracked and he took a deep breath, 'cancer of the pancreas. We can't get back for two days, there's a rail strike and I can't get a seat on a plane. I need you to go and visit right away.'

'When was she admitted?'

'Yesterday evening. She was having tests but her temperature shot up suddenly and they weren't happy with her blood pressure so they took her in straight away.'

'So that's why she didn't come to Angelo's.'

'What?'

'Oh, nothing, sorry. It's just we were meant to meet and then she didn't come and I— Anyway. She wants to see me, you say. You're sure about that?'

'It's your duty, Harriet.' He recited, then repeated, the name and the address of the hospital, of the ward, but Harriet had scant need of his inaccurate directions, his patronising little asides about the local flower vendor and the best fruit shop for her morning berries. It was all too familiar. It was the hospital where she had volunteered.

'We can't get back until Thursday,' he said. 'Can you go and see her in the morning?'

'All right,' Harriet agreed, doubtfully. 'All right, if you think that's what should be done.'

'For God's sake,' he allowed himself this final vent. 'What's wrong with you?'

How long, she did not ask, have you got?

The night passed slowly. The mattress taunted her, bulging and drooping in all the wrong places, like the most basic adversary. Harriet flung open the windows to let out the failing air, but the street noises – the choir of cheerful drunks outside Drinkers Paradise en route for the shelter, weighing up their chances for they were only allowed in half gone and no more, the breathless chatter of teenage girls on telephones to other teenage girls – was too involving for sleep.

She thought of her mother lying in a thin white hospital bed. She would go to her humbly and in her mildest incarnation. Her collapse at Angelo's seemed to her now like a scene from ancient history. She would take her water and some choice fruit and elegant flowers and try as best she could not to grate. Of course she would create no scenes as the minutes ticked! Her mother would be still, breathing effortully, fingers laced stiffly at her breast, eyes closed, with no powers. They had reached this far in their life together, if it wasn't laughable to call it that, without either of them ever mentioning what had passed between them.

If there are things to say you need to say, say them now, do them now, Harriet thought.

Half asleep she pictured the four – mother, father, sister, brother – seated on a makeshift stage beneath a television studio's searching glare. The host eyed them over with knowing sympathy, bobbing about between the rickety platform and the audience's bank of tip-up seats. She'd already been, she always said, to Hell and some of the way back, and it was only half past ten! The show would be taped in half an hour. It was time to warm up the audience. The host's baggy jacket was flapping wildly, sizes too big; she had never felt the same about herself since the twins' father left.

She wanted the audience divided. A fight always made for a better show. Who are the goodies here? Who are the baddies? How would you feel if it was happening in your home? Cheers and jeers. Cheers and jeers, strange to say, sounded almost identical when you were on TV. As long as there was passion and outrage and gasps and the odd chuckle. Looks accounted for an awful lot – of course a sense of humour, everyone wanted that. She would win them over, get them eating out of her hands, cajole her family into a series of historic U-turns possibly. To have the wrongs that others did you recited on air with pink lights and air-brushed skin, hair controlled by whole canisters of lacquer, and advertisements. Miss McGee would have a fit if she found out – a silent, highly controlled one that no one but herself would detect. The products that her ridiculous little skirmishes could help to shift!

Happy Hour

Harriet lingered at the mouth of the hospital, gazing past the ailing brick to the brilliant sky. Clutching her three fresh-green punnets of raspberries, the brown bag full of American cherries, the six perfect apricots, the two bunches of white tulips, their stalks squeaking against the cellophane, she mouthed the words *Good morning* to the day.

And there, weary-seeming on the steps suddenly was Flora's mother! In a loosely belted light-coloured coat she was hand in hand with a taller, broader version of herself. This second woman stood nervously at the other's side, handsome in an old pair of blue jeans and a faded Breton jersey, with silky, wayward gold cropped hair. Sophie – it couldn't not be. She was striking to look at, yellow and pink, her gaze even at a distance of twenty feet startlingly direct. In fact she dazzled wildly in the morning sunshine, astonishingly healthy-looking with none of the dark streaks, the green or pale mauve shadows you might expect on the inmate of an inner city psychiatric ward. She was farm-fresh, haywainish, seasidy, electric, rhubarb and custard even. The more sophisticated sister was a big nothing beside her.

Sophie drew out a pack of cigarettes and lit one, snapping off the filter and throwing it on the ground. She folded her legs beneath her and sat on the top step to smoke. Flora's mother turned suddenly. 'Hello there!' she called to Harriet and with the movement of her features her good looks came somehow more into play.

'Oh, hello.' Harriet bounded over the steps to greet them properly. She turned very slightly towards the sister. 'Hello,' she said, 'I'm Harriet.' The sister nodded and smiled and offered Harriet a cigarette. 'Oh, how nice, but I mustn't!' Harriet murmured cheerfully. It was what she had once heard an orthodox Jewish woman say when offered a thoughtless sausage roll.

'What brings you here?' Sophie asked.

'I'm just going to visit someone.'

'Not one of the girls from school?' Flora's mother asked.

'Oh, no. A relative.'

Sophie unfolded one of her long, strong arms and gave Harriet a very delicate stroke on the head, for consolation.

'Thank you!' Harriet blurted.

Flora's mother raised her brows. 'This is my sister Sophie.'

'This is where I live.' Sophie gestured to the hospital. There was a psychiatric wing in the old building; Harriet had seen the signs.

'How do you do? Harriet Mansfield.' Harriet smiled again. 'From the school,' she told her.

'Of course you are!' Sophie nodded and grinned.

'Anyway, I suppose I'd better not be late. Great to see you both. Isn't the sunshine spectacular? Will you excuse me? Goodbye.' The women all smiled. 'Do let me know if there's anything you need,' she added vaguely as though she were some species of hostess.

In the clanking tin interior of the passenger lift Harriet hummed herself a Christmas carol. Her mother was in Peters ward, in a small private room. A nurse directed her. Outside she stood in preparation for ... for what? She raised her hand to knock but the door swung open and a black nurse in a royal blue tunic emerged, rattling a three-tier trolley. 'Visitor for you, Mrs G!'

'Hello, Ma,' Harriet said, settling her purchases on the bedside stand. 'Can I come in, or ...'

Her mother mouthed an inaudible sound and fluttered the fingers of the nearest hand. Her right wrist was hooked up by means of a short white wire to a bloated bag of pale liquid hanging from a tall stand. There was a chain of bruising up her arm and her fingers were swollen. On her other hand a sort of plastic clothes peg linked her to a heart monitor that charted rows of small regular red hills on a navy screen.

The arms that lay on the pale coverlet were so reduced, the veins standing out, greeny-blue. It's very very serious, Harriet broke the news gently to herself. What she must have been through. A tear splashed on to Harriet's wrist. The despair on her mother's face, in her eyes and in the set of her mouth. To be ill in this way, utterly prone and powerless, it was obviously a great deal more than she could bear. You mustn't let her see how bad it is, Harriet told herself. You must not cause her any more distress. Better to leave now than for her to see in your face how she looks. Yet with sorrow and pain entwined on this scale you fooled yourself by thinking your presence had any sort of—

'How you feeling?' Harriet said very carefully.

The patient could not speak and simply moved her fingers again with great effort. Harriet took her mother's hand very gently in her own. It was freezing cold. She felt something in her mother relax and a small seam of warmth passed between them. Does she even know who I am?

She drew off her coat and spread it out on the bed. She took a seat at the bedside, where she wished her mother well, strenuously, for almost an hour, until interrupted by the same nurse. 'I'm meant to feed her some soup.' She hovered with the tray held at chest height.

'I'll do it,' Harriet said, receiving the tray and setting it down on a small table beneath the window. Next to the soup – which was pale grey-green – there was a heavily buttered poppy-seed roll and a spoon. Her mother's eyes were closed now; she was sleeping. 'I'll wait until she wakes,' Harriet said into the room, covering the soup bowl with the underplate. The roll she wrapped up in the napkin, tucking in the edges.

Her mother did not wake for three hours. The time passed slowly with Harriet tidying, noiselessly, the little room, and sitting on a low chair without feeling or thought. It was very hot. The poor tulips couldn't take it. It was hotter even than the children's ward below. Her mother's sleep sounded peaceful, but her colour was very bad.

When she came to, Harriet managed to spoon a little soup into her mouth, supporting her mother's loose-necked head in a soft tilt so the liquid could drip down her throat. There was a smell in the room of soured meat; the odour of cancer, was it? Two rivulets seeped out of her mother's mouth's corners and on to her chin. Horrified, Harriet apologised gently and dabbed at them; the feel of her fingers on her mother's face shocked her, the skin so thin there was danger of tearing. She placed more soup into her mother's mouth, and more, but the mouth filled and overflowed. Was she not performing the task with enough caring? When she had cleaned up her mother again and apologised for her own ineptitude, again, she felt the patient's head grow heavy in her palms and she set it down again on the pillow and smoothed the hair, which was frail, almost crisp. She stroked it lightly as her mother drifted in and out of consciousness. 'I need to speak to the doctor right away,' Harriet told the nurse when her head peeped round the door.

'I'll let him know.'

The wiry oncologist, when he was eventually found, was dry and circumspect, spectacles too large for his face, mouth softly set for the delivery of bad news. As he spoke, Harriet took her mother's hand. It was almost impossible to listen, but she gleaned from what he said that they were still searching and searching for something they didn't want to find. It wasn't exactly the end of the world; they were several stages from that, but still it was not at all good.

'She seems so despairing,' Harriet protested quietly.

'That may be the morphine,' the doctor said. So that was something.

She stroked her mother's hand in the gentlest way she knew. She hoped with all her heart that no one could judge this physical need of hers to clasp her mother as any kind of infringement or violation. She thought of the anxious youths of today being instructed by their mentors to gain permission for each successive increase in their sexual advances.

The thin, frazzled tangle of her mother's hair was almost the worst of it. Where had it disappeared to, the shoulder-length mahogany sheen? She replaced the hand on the blanket for a moment with the sudden fear that the pleasure it gave her, the comfort their communion was bringing, might, for her mother, be some sort of murderous depletion. After two minutes she relented and took it up again. If it was any sort of abuse, she justified herself, it was done from love. But wasn't that what people always said? She closed her eyes and her thoughts. More hours passed and the room darkened. Through the window Harriet looked down on some sycamore trees which had lost almost half their leaves. How will it ever be possible for me to have a life if you die, Ma?

She stood and drew the curtains and switched on a low side light. The doctor returned and satisfied himself that the results of some tests performed earlier in the day were better than expected. He shot out some figures but said they were not especially reliable. They were conservative, he said. Forty per cent this or that for two years dropping to twenty then ten. 'At this stage anything could still happen.' There was a minute play of mirth at the edges of his lips. 'It's all very irregular. All the signs point to cancer but we've not yet found any.' He seemed distracted, awkward. Fingers crossed or some other sort of banality he would mutter next. Harriet quizzed him about the pain relief options. 'She's responding well to the drugs,' he said. 'You can see there's little agitation, which is good.'

A new nurse wandered in in white rubber shoes, apologised, then backed out of the room again, shutting the door noisily. The patient's eyes flashed open and stared straight into her daughter's, which were filmed with care. 'Thank you,' she whispered. She nodded in and out of consciousness, in and out. If there are things you want to say perhaps you should say them now, Harriet instructed herself.

'Why not head home and come back in the morning,' the doctor said. 'Get some rest yourself. She's quite comfortable. She's not going anywhere. Someone will check on her every half an hour. She has her bell.' Harriet shook her head and watched him leave the room. She switched off the lamp and sat in the dark at her mother's bedside, their fingers closely entwined. She had not realised her mother's fingers were so long and elegant. Her own were like a carthorse. She closed her eyes and allowed herself a few moments of dream time. Her mother's face was as open and calm as an infant's. She felt, in the dark, her own face, the curve of her cheek, the sharpness of her nose, the small scored parallel lines between her eyebrows. It was all bad angles and swellings and ill alignment. She increased very slightly the pressure on her mother's hand, which clung on to her own. It wasn't just a passive thing, there was will there. 'Don't let go,' Harriet whispered. 'Please don't let go.' She tried to see the situation for what it was, but one idea dwarfed all the other thoughts: it was the loveliest time together they had had for years and years and years.

When morning came the doctor announced it was time for more tests to be done.

'I can come with her, hold her hand?'

'I'm afraid you can't, but if you're back by one o'clock you'll be here before she comes round. She won't miss you.'

Harriet walked away, stumbling slightly. The streets surrounding the hospital were dangerously still, the sky dry and blank. Her clothes felt as though she had been wearing them for a week. What was she even doing? Why was there a smile breaking on her face? She didn't understand, but things were changing. She took a seat in a brightly lit café and ordered some tea for herself and some toast.

Years ago, when discussing with a potential boyfriend what love meant – they were twenty-one and drunk and stranded at a country railway station in the middle of the night, moving closer and closer towards each other, amazed at their own daring – he was officially someone else's only she didn't yet know – her coat wrapped around both their shoulders, stars blazing above them as they waited for the dawn train to rescue them – Harriet began thinking out loud. 'This might sound mad but I always thought that part of love, part of real love, is helping the person you love to have a good death, helping someone to die at peace, without anguish or regrets; helping someone to feel clear when they die, reasonable and calm, making a good ending ...' The boy gazed at her intently then moved away, dropping her hand, shuffling to the far end of the bench taking her coat with him. 'Fucking hell, Harriet,' was all he would say, shaking his head from side to side. 'Fucking hell,' he repeated, drawing out a cigarette, his fingers trembling so much that he snapped it in half and of course it was his last one – Sod's Law – so he tried to build a little splint for it with a strip torn from the back of the packet and a twist of silver paper, but that too failed.

School would be opening now, the pupils traipsing up the front steps: scholarly Isabella, Lucy frank and sane, Flora like one's very nicest aunt. She had already talked Honey and Serena through the plans for the week. They had made it clear they could manage supremely well without her, albeit at a courteous notch below. Harriet left the café and returned to the hospital. As she approached the wide pale steps she saw Flora's mother and her sister sitting and chatting, the patient drawing concentratedly on an unlit cigarette. Pleased to see them Harriet wandered over, before, even, they had caught sight of her.

'Hello again!' the sister greeted her warmly, rubbing her head in friendship as she had done formerly. 'Hello! Hello!'

'Hello there,' Harriet answered her. 'Hello.' They were all, suddenly, laughing.

'You remember my sister Sophie?'

'Oh yes,' Harriet said.

'Honey told me about your mother. How is she?' Flora's mother asked.

'She's not dying, they say. Which is, obviously, good. I don't really know how to do this but it was wonderful being with her. They're doing more tests this morning, but I can go back again at lunchtime, they say. They've made her quite comfortable. She can barely talk or move but we hold each other's hands. I didn't realise she had such beautiful fingers. It's very cosy, somehow.' Harriet stopped.

'They keep that place like an oven,' Flora's mother said.

'It's so the germs can grow,' the sister said. 'Can I tell you something nice? We're having haddock mornay for lunch with minted new potatoes.'

'Oh, how delicious.'

'Everyone's very excited.'

'Of course! Haddock mornay is haddock mornay.'

'They put a tiny bit of nutmeg in, but you can really taste it. It makes a world of difference to the flavour. I got a nutmeg grater in a Christmas cracker once. Took a bit of skin off my thumb.'

'Oh no! What bad luck.'

'Christmas is always lovely and terrible. It's traditional.'

'Oh yes, that's exactly right! And do they offer you a pudding?'

'Well today, it says on the thing, castle pudding, but no one seems to know what that is.'

'I think it's with sponge and jam,' Harriet said. 'I'm not certain though. That might be cabinet pudding.'

'My friend was in a hospital in south London and they had scones every Sunday *and* iced butter curls.'

'Well, maybe we should all head down there.'

'Now?'

'I think she was joking,' Flora's mother said.

'Were you joking?'

'Well, I shouldn't joke about something as important as scones. Actually I do know a joke about scones.'

Sophie beamed.

Harriet said, 'What's the fastest cake in the world? Ssscccone!'

Flora's mother looked at her watch. 'I suppose we'd better get you back in. It's half eleven and you don't want to miss your cod.' They all entered the building in a little procession, Harriet leading.

She took the lift up to her mother's floor, strode the fluorescent corridor to her mother's room, gave a knock on the door, pushed it open, took in the tightly made bed, the ribbed plastic pitcher of water and the childish beaker, the thin white light at the window – the last sheen of summer – and the dark ivy clinging to the opposite wall beside an elegant metal fire escape, and sat down in the bedside chair to wait.

Two hours later her mother was brought back asleep, and professionally placed, by two strong men, back into the bed that Harriet hurriedly unfurled for them. She did not even wake when the drips were reattached. Her hands had swollen slightly; the right was fat and pink. 'Can I speak to the doctor now?' Harriet asked.

'He'll speak to you both once she's awake. It shouldn't be long.'

The day wore on. Harriet moved her chair a little closer and took her mother's hand again. Where was the harm? When the patient woke, she looked surprised to see herself in her bed. 'Where am I please?' she asked.

'You're in hospital, Ma. You've been having tests because of some awful pains you've been having. They're trying to get to the bottom of it. The doctor's coming in a moment and he'll fill us in. Colin and Maggie are on their way from Toulon but there's some sort of strike. Do you think you could manage some soup?'

'What are you doing here?'

'I – I thought it wouldn't be nice for you to be on your own in a strange place when you weren't feeling a hundred per cent.'

'What?'

'I came to see how you are.'

'Oh.'

'How you feeling?'

'Never mind about that.'

'Well . . . '

'But what about the girls?' Her voice was uncertain.

'What girls?'

'The ones in your school. Who's taking care of them?'

Harriet was stunned for a moment. 'Oh, nothing to worry about there. I've got a team of four helpers who all do the job excellently. Honey, Linda, Tina and Serena.'

Her mother peered down at her right hand, whose fingers tightly clasped her daughter's. She was getting her bearings, her eyes darting to the ceiling to the mustard-hued carpet to the feeble watercolour on the wall. They rested back again on the place where she and her daughter joined. Her lip curled slightly. Harriet braced herself for what was to come, a brisk shaming separation about which she must betray no signs of being sad.

'Pardon my stupidity, but are we in Paris or London do you know?' she whispered.

'London,' Harriet said.

'Ah.'

'I'm so sorry it's not more elegant. The room.'

'Hardly your fault!' her mother smiled, severe. She cleared her throat and sniffed lightly. 'Now tell me. Little rows of desks? I'm trying to picture . . . a recorder club?'

'Well, we don't really have desks because the children are so little. There are some tables for drawing and doing puzzles, and a sort of large playing room upstairs with a play house and dressing-up things and dolls and cars, and then we do cookery downstairs and upstairs is the art department and there are small carpentry benches with balsawood. And there's a lovely garden where we grow things to eat and flowers for the hall. There's a piano on the ground floor because we love singing. They're a bit young for recorders, I think, but perhaps I'm wrong. I'll look into it. Oh, and tap dancing . . .'

'Oh, delightful. Photographs?'

'No, not with me.'

'Can you bring some in?'

'If you like.'

Her mother lay still for a moment and closed her eyes. Her skin was a warmer colour, she had a little more energy and there was something stronger in her face which the previous day had seemed so frayed. Harriet shut her own eyes down for a second. She has absolutely forgotten that she doesn't like me. Then – with fear – does she actually think I'm someone else?

'I learned nothing at school.' Her mother was speaking again. 'Except how to put up with things.'

'Oh no!' Harriet said. 'How awful, although, I mean, I don't know, perhaps you think that was a good thing to learn. Or would you rather they had taught you to, you know, kick up a stink?'

Her mother laughed. 'Kick up a stink!' she said with delight. 'You say the funniest things.'

The 'you' was a sort of you plural. How has she grouped me? Harriet wondered. 'What sort of things did you have to put up with anyway, at school? Nothing too bad, I hope?'

'Well, the usual things, not enough food, cold ...' Her face darkened and she shivered. 'Spiteful nuns.'

'Oh no!' Harriet heard herself say. 'Were yours especially un—?'

'But your thing sounds heavenly.'

'I do hope so.'

'I expect' – she was struggling for breath now – 'they don't know they're born!'

Harriet smiled.

'Did you mention something about soup?' her mother said.

'Yes, I'll arrange it, Ma. Won't be a second.' Finally, she undid their hands, with almost more regret than she could bear. There will be other times, she promised herself blithely, only half believing.

At the door she met the doctor again, who was on his way in. He stepped on her foot, but it did not hurt, and he didn't apologise or even seem to take it in.

'My mother would like some soup,' she said grandly.

'That's good. I'll ask the nurse to bring something in a moment. Well, there's good news all round it seems. Thus far, we can't find any cancer. That's not to say there absolutely isn't any, because your symptoms suggest it, but we can find nothing internally that supports the view that you do have cancer. Nothing at all.'

'What is causing all the pain then?'

'It's pancreatitis, as we first thought. An acute inflammation, and the stomach lining is in bad shape. The spleen's not good. But you're responding excellently to the drugs. The news, at this point, really couldn't be better.' He reached forward and patted Harriet's mother's head. She stiffened and pursed her lips.

Some time later the nurse arrived with a tray. There was grey soup and some cold grey-white fish and a little stack of snipped greyish green beans. 'Need me to feed you?' the nurse asked, swinging out the arm of the bedside table unit so that it made a bridge of food across the bed.

'No thank you very much, dear.' There was the familiar note of ice. The *dear* was really a slap. Pride bloomed in Harriet's heart and she busied herself behind her mother's head, rearranging the pillows so that there was more support for her shoulders and neck.

'Thanks.'

'You know yesterday you couldn't even manage soup.'

'Couldn't I? I do feel much better. That doctor's pretty full of himself. And how old can he be? Twenty-eight?'

'Although wonderful to have a doctor who says "Thus far."'

'Yes, that is true . . . it's good you are here.'

'It's an enormous pleasure for me.' It was.

'Now, after I've had my lunch, I think I'd like you to get back to your girls. I feel awfully guilty keeping you away. I can hardly play hopscotch with you, can I? You can pop back in the morning.'

'Perhaps I'll just look in this evening, if I may.'

'Well, that would be extremely nice.'

'There are some raspberries and apricots in the little cupboard. I brought them yesterday but they should still be all right.'

'Very kind. And er – if it doesn't seem terribly eccentric, please salute them for me, would you, your charges?'

'Of course!'

On the hospital steps Harriet began whistling, her lips a little concentrated hoop of glee. The tune was old fashioned, wistful, debonair, a mannish boast, luxurious, carefree. It was only when she neared the chorus that her head shook wryly and with embarrassment. She stopped whistling and instead began singing.

I'm putting all my eggs in one basket.
I'm betting everything I have on you.
I'm saving all my love for one baby,
Heaven help me if my baby don't come through.

Just be a bit careful, all right? she said to herself gently. In the distance Miss McGee's face shimmered with approval. Harriet took herself squarely in hand. It won't last, I know it won't, and everything will turn sour again and awful again and things will get unbearably cold, so let me just enjoy it blindly now. I know it's foolish, but I still need good news. I won't take it for more than it is. Can't I just enjoy it for what it is? Can't I, can't I please, in case the actual ending isn't any good?

Opening the front door of the school with her key Harriet felt unrecognisable: softer, milder, more carefree, as though some central wire that ran right though her had been changed for a scrap of yellow wool. It was one p.m. The girls' voices could be heard from the garden, where there was general merrymaking surrounding the planting of a tiny apple tree. 'Hello, everyone,' Harriet said, leaning against the willow in the sunshine, batting its frankly too friendly leaves away from her face. 'I'm sorry I've not been much here. My mum was ill, but she's a bit better now.' She could think of no more words to say.

'Let me make you a cup of tea,' Honey offered. Linda brought Harriet a garden chair.

Some of the girls folded themselves down at Harriet's feet, then stretched out their limbs in the sunlight. 'You need to look after people when they're having a difficult day. That's what kind is,' Alice was announcing to her circle.

'And jokes,' Mia said. 'All right, so a man went to the doctor because he had five willies.'

'Goodness,' Harriet said.

'The doctor said, "But how on earth do you do your knickers on in the morning?"'

The man said, '"Well, it's okay because what I do is, I usually wear a glove."'

'Oh, very good,' Harriet said, 'if rather—'

'Harriet must be tired after her long night. She needs to rest,' Linda said firmly.

'Tell us a story about hospitals please, a made-up story,' Isabella said. 'With doctors in white coats.'

'And medication,' Flora added.

'And people having their bad legs chopped up,' Alice pressed.

Harriet smiled. 'My goodness. Let's think. I know—' but Honey appeared at her side.

'Did I tell you what happened when Eggs and Bacon had to have their tonsils out?' she asked.

And in the late afternoon Honey came to find Harriet who was snoozing on the upper floor. She knocked and handed her a cup of tea and a misshapen bun. 'How are things?' she asked.

'The thing is I just don't know.'

At six o'clock Harriet returned to the hospital, calling the lift with three extravagant squeezes of the illuminated square button. She settled into its forlorn tin interior; its repeated rusty clanks did make you fear for its health. In her arms was a large brown cardboard box containing a package from Angelo's she had collected en route, a foil-wrapped plate bearing a majestic grilled Dover sole and some plain steamed spinach and green beans that she had ordered.

There was a lemon upholstered in white muslin and some stewed blackberry and apple with no sugar in a small cut-glass bowl.

Harriet knocked at her mother's door.

'Hello?'

Her mother was sitting up in bed in a pale blue nightgown dotted with tiny pink roses like some kind of antique May Queen. She was eating some smoked salmon finger sandwiches from a white polystyrene box, and next to that was a green cardboard punnet of French strawberries.

'Hello?' Harriet said with a questioning smile. Her mother did not reply but motioned with her hand that she would answer when her mouth was not so full. Her skin tone was visibly brighter, her spirits also. She had shrugged off some more of her invalid's pallor, her weak gestures, the fluttering that seemed to go on at her delicate extremities. The new nightgown revealed her fresher aspects. Had someone been brushing her hair?

Harriet set the supper box on the floor and came and sat in the bedside chair. In the apple green velour seat pad there was definitely some sort of indentation, she thought as she sat. The seat was warm!

Just then the door opened and Harriet's brother's wife walked in.

'Hello, Maggie,' Harriet said smoothly.

'Harriet.'

'Maggie brought me this beautiful nightdress.'

'Well, the hospital ones were so dismal. We couldn't bear to see her in one of those . . . Positively soul-destroying. By the way, thank you,' Maggie went on, 'so much for holding the fort.'

The door moved again and this time Colin entered. 'Oh, Harriet,' he said, as though even her name were a sort of curse.

'Hello, Colin.' The little room was crowded now.

'What's in the box?' Colin asked, almost stepping on it.

'Some fish and vegetables,' Harriet said. 'For supper.'

'But you've eaten your sandwiches, haven't you, Mother?'

'Well . . . perhaps I could manage a mouthful—'

'Please don't worry,' Harriet said, 'I can easily take it away again.'

'Perhaps you'd have it, Colin,' his mother asked.

'If it would help, I suppose I—'

'You can't be hungry, surely,' Maggie said. 'We didn't have lunch till three. We could take it back for the cats, perhaps?'

'Will you excuse me a second,' Harriet asked. She went out into the corridor and sauntered over to the nurses' station, which was unattended. She helped herself to a cup of water from the water cooler. Presently she was joined by Maggie.

'What's the matter now?' Maggie asked.

'The man who makes the mats.'

'What?'

'The fellow who makes the mats.'

Maggie began again. 'Isn't it wonderful to see her so much better?'

'Yes. Yesterday I almost thought she—'

'Colin spoke to the doctor at length yesterday from the airport and he filled us in.'

'Right.'

'If you're tired, do head home because we're well rested and more than happy to—'

'I'm fine.'

Maggie took a sip from a polystyrene cup. 'I don't want to be rude, but I think family tension is the last thing that's needed at the moment so it probably really would be best if you—'

'I just can't listen to things like that,' Harriet said.

Maggie took a step back. 'Still angry.'

'You're wrong, I'm not angry. I'm actually extremely well. Life is good.'

Maggie gave a little dismissive snort.

'I'm not angry in the least,' she continued – but it was one of those things you could never ever prove. 'Things are going really well.'

'But everything about you is simply *inflamed* with grievances.' The epithet had not a fresh sound to it, Harriet remarked to herself. She had been storing that one, you could tell; she could almost hear its echoes rehearsed between the two of them in their mindless tailored shorts on the golf course or the quoits pitch. Besides, Harriet mused, she wouldn't say that to me if I didn't have red hair. Two nurses passed and installed themselves at computers behind the ledge against which Harriet and her sister-in-law were leaning.

'Look, I can see you haven't had things properly explained, but it may interest you to know that I forgave and forgot everything years ago. Although what business it is of yours—'

'Yes, but you drag your forgiveness round like a great weapon.'

'I do what?'

'I'm quite sure you heard me.'

'I'm finding it hard to believe my ears.'

'Are you threatening me?'

'Shh.' Harriet spoke softly, as though comforting a wailing child. 'Shh now. Please. Remember where we are. Do try to be calm. These things are very stressful. It's all right.' And suddenly their odd conversation, their vitriolic little dance, was dead.

They went back into the patient's room. Her mother and brother were deep in a conversation which they halted abruptly. Harriet asked her mother, asked her brother, if there was anything further that they needed. They shook their heads. Nothing they needed, or rather 'We have everything we need' was what they said. Her brother rose from his seat and began to bid her goodbye, although she had made no motion to leave.

'I'm so glad you're feeling better,' Harriet said. Her mother gave a gracious little bed bow. Then, because it was inevitable, she told them what they wanted to hear. 'I expect I ought to be getting back.' Her mother nodded again. 'Goodbye,' Harriet said and she blew a large purely friendly kiss on her palm to them all, right across the room.

She would return in the morning, get her mother on her own. They would have to go home, sooner or later, the children would miss them, wouldn't they? Wouldn't they? She imagined Robin and Caroline ecstatic in the hands of some temporary minder, a local girl who actually allowed them to do things, who let them say and feel and be and eat things!

Flora's mother was on the hospital steps alone, sipping from a bottle of water, weary and forlorn. 'How's the patient?' she asked Harriet straight away.

'Oh, definitely on the mend. The doctor's amazed at her progress.'

'Oh. I thought the news might be bad because you look sad.'

'Oh no, just thoughtful I suppose. And what news of Sophie?'

'Not good. She – well, there was trouble last week. She's back in Davis ward. Even the duty nurse, who's normally quite unflappable, said it was a good thing it happened in a hospital.'

'I'm so sorry.'

'The awful thing is I feel so angry and let down.'

'Of course you do. It's a terrible thing to have hanging over you.'
The word hanging! How could she?

But the woman did not seem to mind. 'Of course it doesn't have the same sort of emergency as when it happens the first time. I mean it's still a bit— Oh, I don't know. She didn't want me to go this evening. She held on to my arm. Flora didn't want me to go either. She was screaming and she actually bit my wrist – it didn't hurt—'

'Flora did?' Harriet couldn't imagine.

'No, no, sorry, Sophie.'

'Nice to be in demand though,' Harriet said.

'I know I haven't handled things well.'

'Does the hospital offer any advice about all this?'

'Not really. They're very nice, of course, but – oh, I don't know.'

'What does your husband think?'

'He wants us to have another child but I just think we can't. Not with things as they are.'

'You think it would finish her off?'

'I'm not being silly but it might. When Flora was born, she was terrible. Sophie was. It felt as though I was trying to kill her. Or – or she was trying to kill me. Miles was furious, which didn't help. It was the same at our wedding. I thought the pain I was giving her by getting married actually might not be worth it.'

'I'm so sorry,' Harriet said again.

'Thank you.' Flora's mother drew herself back a little. 'It's just something that happens, every now and then in my life, really. The doctor says I should wait until the New Year and see how things are then. Can I ask you something different? It's about Lucy from school.'

'Of course.'

'She came round for tea at the weekend, Flora and I made a cake specially, and when it got to six o'clock I expected her mother or the nice nanny to fetch her but no one came. Then it was seven and half seven and I rang all the numbers we had but nobody answered. It was very odd. In the end she stayed for a sleepover. I made sure it was fun for them – they had a very early midnight feast and so on – and then the next morning about eleven the nanny came for her, full of excuses that didn't sound at all convincing, not to either of us. It did worry me a bit. Even Miles thought it was strange.'

'Thank you. Thank you very much for telling me. At the moment things are a bit unclear. But it's very helpful to know these things.'

They made their goodbyes slightly awkwardly, on more formal terms.

Just then she saw her brother and her brother's wife walking away from the hospital also, deep in conversation, in the direction of the bleakest local coffee shop. Or rather her brother was talking, victoriously and with some animation, while his wife's eyes were fixed on the ground. She looked ailing and forlorn, her equanimity, her unfailing neatness suddenly striking her observer like an absence rather than a triumph. Her attack had been disgusting, Harriet admitted, but it was, none the less, impressive. It was from the heart.

'Colin!' she called out. 'Maggie!' but they did not hear or if they did they did not turn.

She waited, Harriet Mansfield, until they were quite out of sight before darting back into the hospital. She ran up three flights of stairs to her mother's room and lingered at the door. The corridor was busy. After half a minute she knocked and entered and lowered her eyes to meet the elderly patient's in the bed.

'Oh, hello,' her mother said dully. 'I thought everyone had gone.'

'Just popped back, really, to see if there was anything else you needed. At all.'

'No, I don't think so. Maggie brought me this lovely nightie. It's got roses.'

'I know, it's lovely and cheering.'

'She's such a thoughtful person. She even helped me brush my teeth. Caroline and Robin made get well cards.'

Harriet took a small step back into the room. 'I was wondering if you would like me to read to you? I've got some books in my bag.'

'Oh no, dear. I don't think so. A bedtime story? At my age?'

'You're no age at all, Ma.'

'The last time I was in hospital was when you were born.' Her mother shook her head. 'I only want another year.'

Harriet was silent. A year! Would that give her time to . . . to . . .

'I'm just about to fall asleep, if you don't mind. Could you switch off the lights? *Comme je suis fatiguée*, as they say. They seem to find excuses to disturb me every five minutes asking me things, seeing if I want anything, when all I want is sleep.'

'Who, your visitors?'

'No, the nurses, the cleaners, the medicine people, the staff.'

'I'll pop out and have a word with them at the desk, tell them you're settling down for the night and to leave us alone.'

'Oh, would you, dear? That would be a great help.'

'I'll sit here,' Harriet said, 'while you doze off. Then I'll go and tell the nurse. It will be cosy,' she ventured. She stood and drew the curtains gently, then snapped off the lights. The room was pitch black.

'Is that too dark for you, or—'

'No, I like the dark.'

'And there's nothing else you need?'

'No, dear.' Was there a faint note of irritation?

'All right then. Good night. Sweet dreams. It's wonderful to see you so much better.'

'All right, dear. Very good.' She paused for a moment. 'You're a good girl.'

'Thanks, Ma.' And then, seconds later, her mother's nostrils gave a little dry snort and by the even sound of her breathing Harriet could tell she was asleep.

After a little while, Harriet stood and parted the curtains very slightly so that a thin chink of street light made it possible to see. Her mother's unconscious head looked small and vulnerable on the coarse pillow casing, her parched hair extending out behind her. Perhaps tomorrow she would fetch some more luxurious linen and they would see about washing her hair. Harriet examined the lines on her mother's face, which were deep and smooth. They glistened slightly in the half-light where a night cream containing orchid extract had been applied. The skin on the eyelids was soft, almost transparent, the eyelashes colourless, the cheekbones still sheer and high. *That nightdress is too girlish for her. It takes no account of her serious disposition; there's no dignity in its all-over floral print, its springy frilled placket.* Harriet shook her head with some anger. It was a callous garment for an ageing invalid, gaudy and crass.

Silently she exited the room and walked over to the nurses' station. The fair-haired nurse from yesterday was doing a word search puzzle where all the words were desserts. SUNDAE she had ringed in blue biro. SYLLABUB. 'My mum's sleeping now, so if no one could disturb her?' The nurse nodded agreeably. A phone call came through with a repressed night-time ring tone. Harriet lingered. The nurse took some news, her 'rights' and her 'yeses' intelligent and reassuring, but she barely responded to the caller otherwise. She replaced the receiver and took up her top lip in her teeth.

'Everything all right?'

'I'm glad I'm down here on geriatrics. I used to be up on Williams ward, but they rotated me. I wasn't handling the stress. I felt I was always about to snap. I told my line manager and she said that's the way we all feel. What makes you think you're so different? But she did listen. She's good like that.'

'Oh, good.'

'Your mother, she's a model patient. Never complains, always says thank you. No trouble at all really. Will you be heading off now she's asleep?'

'No, I'll sit with her a bit longer. I don't like to leave her alone.'

'You should go and get some sleep yourself.'

'I know, but . . . but . . . I don't like to miss anything. I'll sit with her tonight. I can snooze in the chair. It's not uncomfortable.'

The nurse nodded.

'Besides, this is the best we've been for years, her and me I mean.'

The nurse paused and seemed to weigh her words before speaking. 'A lot of people find they can have a bit of a fresh start in here.' She nodded, pleased with her diagnosis, with her theorising. 'It's good really, I suppose.'

Harriet could only agree.

'I'll pop back in to my mother now, make sure everything's okay. Do you know what the time is?'

'It's coming up for half eight.'

Harriet crept back into the room where her mother still slept, and flopped in the side chair. She made a brief inventory of all she could see in the dryish gloom: the unpromising plant, the water carafe and the glass and the spare glass, the extra nightdress folded on the window ledge – this time with purplish flowers, vein-violet – the wicker basket lined with waxy-looking apples, red and green.

Through the window the view was unaltered, the ivy and the fire escape and unlit, sleeping roofs. Her mother's sleeping was almost soundless. She had safeguarded her dignity, her aloofness, well in ill health. Harriet blinked at the old lady lying there, her body recovering rapidly in the dark. Its contours had softened slightly, some sharpness had been drained from her system, but these things too might be perceived as symptoms which would themselves heal with time. A police siren went by, slicing the silence, and her mother's shoulder stirred, loosening the covers from an arm that was thick with mauve bruising. Harriet stood and folded the blanket back in place. She tucked it tenderly under the thin mattress so it wouldn't fall again. The skin was warm and creased and dotted with pale freckles. She looked, Harriet felt strongly, gazing at the mouth, the lips thin and pale and parched and lightly open, as though she could not hurt a fly.

If there are things you need to say, she told herself again, say them now. It would not matter if they went unheard. They would linger in the air. It would be a reasonable compromise. But there was nothing to say. There was barely, even, anything to think. The traffic's muted roar beneath the window soothed and comforted. Harriet stretched out her long and handsome limbs contentedly. In a party dress, aged twenty-two once, her companion had told her she looked like a distinguished colonel got up in drag. She had turned her face away to hide her tears. How did humans have the energy to be that hostile to people they did not even like? She shook her head.

The night wore on and Harriet, in her easy chair, resisted sleep. Something about the basic inequality of things was troubling her, her mother lying unconscious in the little bed while she herself flashed and bristled with feelings, almost livelier than life.

Something about her own safety felt uncertain. Her mother shifted in her sleep and licked her lips, and round her eye sockets, at the corners of her mouth, Harriet saw small marks of cruelty.

She stood up and shot out into the corridor. There were no nurses at the hexagonal station but a lone male cleaner told her there were cafés on the upper floors where she might buy a sandwich and a tea. There were spots of blood on his overalls.

'Want me to keep half an eye?' the cleaner asked.

'Would you?'

'Not a problem.'

Instead of to the upstairs café Harriet led herself down in the lift and through the thick doors and outside on to the pale hospital steps. She wanted moonlight and the odour of the streets. She watched the cars passing, the road streaked with colour and lights. She sat down, her legs and arms ungainly as though she had been splattered against the smooth concrete. Twenty feet away a clutch of smokers stood, some attached by clear tubes to companionable-looking mobile drip units. She tried to think things through but everything was strain and confusion – she must close down her thoughts for the night. She was so tired she thought she might vomit. Her head was bad; her breathing, her pulse, and all the mechanical operations and processes whose job it was to keep an ordinary human person ticking over were difficult and painful. Effort was required for even the merest—

And suddenly, she didn't know what she was capable of. Her head filled with desperate crimson images. They danced, almost merrily, these horrible ill-lit scenes in the back of her brain as though they were the mildest human wishes. And the questions that accompanied them, dreadful pitiless things.

What, in this unprecedented situation, counted as personal

safety? She must not go back to that room; there was too much responsibility there. A mother passed with two sulky young children attempting to keep up with her brisk pace. She scolded them sharply and tried to hurry them along, yanking at the hand of the older one until the child yelped and clutched at her armpit. Harriet winced. She saw herself standing, cowering, before a terrible scene, tidying and arranging things. How did you not leave clues?

She wished her mother would wake and they could face each other as friends again. There would be failures as the night progressed: small trails of saliva would spill and dry into chalky paths round her mother's mouth. Her eyes would crust, the lids and lashes sticky with granular deposits. She might leak fluids from her nose and in the morning there would be the question of using the bed pan or the lavatory, if no accidents had already declared themselves. To monitor these developments, to stay kind and loving, to resist and refuse any sharp impulse for a reckoning – would you call it? – might it be just too much to ask? For a second Harriet longed for the habitual exasperated hostility of their ordinary relationship, for just now she had no idea where she stood.

The physical closeness was so bewitching though. She was drawn irresistibly to her mother, to the room where her mother lay prone and childlike in her undignified nightwear as powerfully as— It was just this question of her own innocence that troubled her. Was she really capable of harm? She adored the sound of her mother's breaths, their steadiness, their self-confidence. As a person, she was entirely undefeatable. Remember that, Harriet told herself, and trust yourself. Yet her brother would not trust her alone in that room. God forbid! On that easy chair, he'd shriek, there are two stiff green pillows! (Harriet, too, had noticed them.) Are you insane? He would not allow it. He would be stern at first, then adamant that it was an outrage for his sleeping invalid mother's peace to be invaded in this way. That she should lie unguarded while dangerous persons, armed with delusions and motives, paraded before her with their livid gripes and plights. Well he would not stand for it. He'd manhandle and fault-find. He'd want a full inquiry, he'd terrorise the one in charge and he'd get what he wanted too because *he* was a bully. He'd shoehorn his hapless *relation* into Sophie's ward, range her among the blurred psychiatric cases. He'd inject her with the sedative himself: 'Double the dose, nurse, double the dose.' Sometimes she thought he'd never be happy until she was locked up, quite resigned to her fate (It's for the best; it's for the best all round), in a mental ward. Death row! Cruel to be kind, he would nod sensibly, fooling everyone. That would be his version of heaven, the vast unlovely problem of her solved once and for all. And what was it, ever, she had done?

'Find something to eat,' she told herself. 'Calm down. You are sick with tiredness.' She loved her mother with such an enormous thrust of emotion that the feeling of it, the full force of it throbbing in her body, shaking in her palms, lurching around her with each successive heartbeat, *was* a sort of violence.

She spoke as she might to a child. It is a bit of a crisis, she conceded. You're not quite sure what the best thing is to do. If only there was someone to advise, to shape her actions, to stop her. If only there were Honey and Linda, Tina and Serena sanguine and strapping in their crazy clothes, their glossy-messy hairstyles, their paint mixing and song singing, their affectionate jokes and the intelligent and eager goodwill that streamed out of their every— She could telephone Honey now or Serena. Honey was unshockable, Harriet had once thought. Could she ring Jim and Daisy, throw herself on their hands?

But it was a chance in a lifetime. She went back into the building, ran into the lift, jabbing at the buttons to carry her faster to her mother's bedside. Her words of reassurance were garbled and alarmed but the message she constantly repeated was this: Listen to me. Walk away. Walk away now and go home. Don't take any unnecessary risks. You're not yourself. You don't know what you're doing. You must protect yourself. But still the lift travelled wheezing up to her mother's floor. But I've never – it was true – hurt another human being in my life. Never in my life, she retorted. Not once. It's not what I do.

At the threshold of her mother's door a male nurse was chatting to the cleaner. 'Hasn't made a peep,' the nurse told her. 'I popped my head round the door, but she's out like a light.'

'Thank you. Very kind.' Harriet opened her bag. Everything was compromising, nail scissors, a ball of string. Her shoulders were trembling and her hands started darting about in the air.

'You all right?'

'Yes,' she said but her face was wet and her palms shook so hard that when she clasped them together the single fist she made could not be stilled. 'It's all getting to me a bit I suppose. Going a bit mad or something.'

'There's a cab number by the pay phone. You're shaking. Did you find something to eat?' The nurse put the back of his hand to her forehead. 'You're freezing cold and it's tropical in here. You need to get yourself home. You're not well. I bet you haven't slept for nights. There's all sorts of bugs here. You can come back tomorrow. She'll sleep through now and if there's any change we'll phone you. Write your number down for me. That's it.'

Harriet could barely take it in. Decisions were being made to have her off the premises. Did they think she was actually capable of— 'I'll call the taxi for you.' And before she had said anything the nurse was ringing for her and booking the car and it would be there in five minutes and they waited ten until a call came through and they were both going down in the lift together and he was opening the door and telling the man her address – it looked like an ordinary taxi, it didn't seem like a trick – and then fifteen minutes later she was standing miraculously on her top step.

'Give us a little wave when you get in, just so we know you're all right,' the driver requested. 'Been one of those days?'

And when her key fitted perfectly into the keyhole and the large door opened for her and she breathed in the dry sweet odour of wax crayons and wet newspaper and wallpaper glue and – was it? – coconut ice, she came back on to the doorstep and lifted up her weary arm and she waved and waved and waved and waved and waved.

When Flora's mother arrived at the school closing-down auction, she barely met Harriet's eye, but how could she not let slip an ironic glance when she raised her hand for the doll's hospital and the remaining medical supplies (32 items)? You could not make it up! Flora was going to Charterbury now, much farther away but there was a smart bus that went from the end of the road at ten to nine. Charterbury's uniform had a hat with a grosgrain ribbon and a blue blazer with gold piping. She saw them in the morning sometimes.

Do they think I'm cracked, this whole room? Harriet wondered. Bet they think I rise each morning now and take a class of ghost girls through their lessons, lead a phantom crocodile through the market to soak up the local colour. Do they imagine me tossing pancakes for seventeen children, squeezing the lemon, doing a tango with the sugar shaker so the grains come out in a mad jazz pattern? She wondered if the looks she got sometimes, and the panicky body swerves of ex-school parents, resembled those meted out to a stunned mother of a stillborn child.

You could see people every day in London, people who had more to cope with than their resources could allow for, struggling to meet the shortfall. It was perfectly normal, but it was awfully sad.

Well, she wasn't as bad as all that! Sometimes she watched the men who used the shelter over the road inject themselves swiftly in doorways before going in for the evening; anything to help them through the night. The relief that hit their faces as the drugs entered their bloodstream. It was like a baby with a bottle.

Well, she didn't pretend she still had pupils. Please! For a split second when she woke she sometimes set out the stall of herself, all singing, all dancing, all glitter and glue sticks, for the coming day, but before a minute was out she always remembered. It was only the ordinary way of grief. She might give the house to the shelter over the road and just keep the top flat for herself. Anyone could see they needed more room and more beds. And more helpers. But everyone said best not make any big decisions for a year. Get through the winter first. Early days.

Better By the Day

The following morning, Harriet invited her staff out to breakfast before the girls arrived. 'My mother gets better by the day,' she said.

They traipsed through the market where a fruiterer was assembling lemons in purple paper, and next to him at the clothing stall a fluttering T-shirt showed an orange stick man with his head between the legs of an orange woman. Underneath, a caption read I LOVE SUSHI.

'Fuck!' Tina exclaimed.

Aren't we getting on well? Harriet thought.

At the café they commandeered the largest table and ordered five Full Englishes. They were oddly dressed today, her staff: Tina in a structured navy jacket, almost a blazer; Serena wearing a knife-pleat skirt, Honey chalk-striped business trousers, Linda a white shirt with Peter Pan collar. In her absence they had reached for a maturer sartorial register, Harriet saw. They looked much more provisional and uncertain in these odd professional clothes but the courtesy of it almost moved her to tears.

Charles from the corner was sitting at a small table at the back of the room – recognisable by his greenish coat tails and his boots – his head cordoned off by spread newspaper sheets.

'First of all a million thanks for looking after things,' Harriet began; she would avoid Maggie's tainted 'holding the fort'. 'And B, how has it been for you all?'

Honey was attempting to tame a pink and red flabby rasher. 'Mainly good,' she said. 'Hyacinth shoots are beginning to show. Mermaid project all finished – those stick-on sequins you ordered have arrived—'

'Oh, the box of Krazy Kwins—'

'Yes, and we've made the mermaids into a mobile on the first floor. We've started on the Tudor palace now; we just need a few more courtiers. Everyone's choosing their favourite wife of Henry! Tina got lots of scraps of brocade from that African stall at the back of the market. Isabella said this morning, "Henry VIII was a wicked man, how else to explain that he killed two of his wives?" Good, isn't it?'

Serena took over the round-up. 'Okay, so we didn't make bread yesterday as I know you were particularly wanting to do it, so we did scones – hope that's okay. Half sultana and half plain, in case you were wondering. We read the Book IX bit from *The Odyssey*. They all staggered round the garden with their eyes shut pretending to be the Cyclops wailing, "No man has wounded me. No man is trying to kill me!" Hilarious! I made a little film. I realise this is hardly life and death stuff,' she said. 'Unless you happen to be a Cyclops.' She chased a charred tomato half round her plate until it wept its pips. 'Some of them thought he was called Norman.'

'Well . . . ' Harriet nodded enthusiastically.

Linda said, 'Genevieve's baby has been born, a little brother called Isadore.'

'How's she taking to it?'

Tina speared a grey sausage coin, garnished it with some beads of scrambled egg, dipped the whole into the juice of the tomato, swallowed it down and wiped her lips on her hanky. 'She says Isadorable!'

'That's excellent. Now tell me what isn't going so well?'

Honey paused, swatting some strands of honey-coloured hair from her plate.

'Lucy's in a bit of a state.'

'Oh no! Has anything happened?'

'That's just it. We don't know. We've spoken to Tessa but none of us know quite what to do, do we? She's been crying an awful lot.'

'Oh dear!'

'We've telephoned her mother a number of times and left messages and emailed but nothing comes back,' Linda said.

'I'll write a letter inviting her in and perhaps we can all have a meeting.'

'She seems very thin on the ground.' Serena looked thoughtful. 'And the father?'

'He's not on any of the forms, so we don't quite like to mention him.'

'Such a shame,' Tina said, shaking her head. 'Whatever's going on, Lucy can't handle it at all.'

'I hate the idea,' Harriet said, 'that children should have to handle anything until they're, well, at least—'

'Twenty-five?' Honey offered. Honey was twenty-five.

'I was going to say thirty-five,' Harriet laughed.

'Not that we've been spying, but she brought quite a lot of food into school yesterday, and started eating in the loos.'

'What sort of food?'

'Slices of plain bread, some cream crackers, cold spaghetti in a box, nothing nice.'

'Poor little thing.'

The girls were silent. Charles came out from behind his newspaper and wandered over to their table.

'Heard your mother was bad. So sorry.'

'She's on the mend. Soon be her old self,' Harriet said crisply. 'Now, I've been meaning to ask you, would you pop in some time and give a little talk to the girls about *The Odyssey*? They are getting quite keen on it. As a sort of job?'

'Why not?'

Harriet stood outside the front door as the children trickled past her, clutching their parents' or each other's hands. In the upstairs playing room later on Flora said, 'My auntie's not well.'

'I'm sorry,' Harriet said. 'Shall we make her a lovely card?'

'It's me that needs people doing a card.'

'I will make one for you, Flora.'

'How is your mother?' Isabella asked.

'Much better, thank you for asking. Now, who wants to help me make the dining table? Carved oak, I thought, and the fireplace? We've got some stick-on gems for the ladies' gowns.'

'I'm doing the feast over here,' Tina said. 'Who wants to help me? I'm doing their pudding made of rose petals on golden dishes and a big plate of capons, like big chickens, stuffed with boiled eggs.'

'Ladies' dresses over here,' Serena called out.

'Who wants to help me do shoes?' Linda said. 'These buckles are very fancy. Should we be doing some poor Tudors as well? What did they wear?'

By ten o'clock there was no evidence of Lucy. Harriet telephoned Tessa.

'I can't really talk right now.'

'Is there anything I need to know?'

'Everything's all— Look, I can't talk. I'll try and phone you later.'

Harriet returned to the main classroom. The tables had been cleared to one side. On the floor there was an outline on white paper of an almost life-size Henry VIII. He was gnawing at a brace of chickens, holding one by the leg in each fist.

'I'm going round there,' Harriet announced. 'I'm not happy. The sun's coming out. Why not put some tents up in the garden and have a sort of camping lunch?'

'I'll get on to it now.' Serena leapt into action.

'Shall I come with you?' Honey offered.

'I'll go alone. I think it's best.'

Harriet walked out of the school and into thin rain. Through a basement window she saw a boy of early teenage, peaky and indulged in tartan dressing gown, pouring milk straight into an open box of cereal. One of the windows above had a faded rug strung up as a makeshift curtain, and over its bowed edge she saw a man, half dressed, frying at a two-ringed stove. The smell of bacon flooded the street. He was muscular and suntanned. A gym bunny, was that the phrase? She turned into the main road.

The nanny is intelligent and kind but she is barely twenty and out of her depth. She realised she had not thought of her mother in more than an hour.

They would discharge her in the next few days, the doctor had said, but she would need looking after. Harriet shook her head. There were brisk private nurses you could bribe to care for you in Paris, as in every capital of the world. They would guarantee not to catch your eye at the more embarrassing moments. They would disappear the second you indicated it was your wish, which certainly could not be said of one's relations. Yet you could not talk to them about things. They would turn away in the face of disclosures or recollections. Might there even be scorn or derision attached to such unnegotiated human appeals, as there might be with a prostitute?

At the junction, Harriet crossed the road recklessly. A driver shouted from a wound-down window, 'Are you insane?' Harriet walked on. She turned into Lucy's street and marched up to her door.

She rang the bell but no answer came. She waited. She rang again. She peered at the upper windows, which were shaded by dark blinds. On the ground floor thick curtains were pulled across the bay. The house seemed hollow. She peered through the letter box. On the floor beneath the front door about fifty letters lay. Harriet fixed her finger over the bell and kept it pressed for a minute. There was no life there. After a while she heard the sound of a window being shunted open at the house next door, a man's voice crying out. Harriet's head swung up.

'Stop that,' he shouted. 'I'm trying to sleep.'

Back in her room, she dialled Tessa's number but it was all *Please leave a message* over ailing country music, a woman pleading with another to leave her no-good husband alone. She would pay her hospital visit now and return to school life in time for lunch, she decided. You must keep things normal for the children, she thought, like a well-balanced divorcee. She took a small glass jar of hyacinths from the mantelpiece that were just coming into bud. Her mother's case did not lie smoothly in her mind.

On the hospital steps, made glossy by the rainfall, she paused to gather herself. There was little chance her mother would be sleeping now. That was a scene she did not care to revisit. A parent's distaste for its child was as natural as its love. It was worth remembering that.

She commiserated with the lift as they both lurched, cranky and graceless, to the upper floors. She clutched the hyacinths to her chest and a little of the water bubbled up and dribbled on her skirt. She dabbed at it roughly with her hand, the liquid thick and sour and flecked with mud. Never mind, she commanded. The lift rattled to a halt and she exited uncertainly, feeling her way along the hospital's bright corridor, breathing in the highly medicated air. Her mind kept darting back to the previous evening. She would never have done anything, anything definitive that could not be undone, however brave she was, however cowardly. She lived in dread of such unique epiphanies.

Outside her mother's door, she saw suddenly that the whole thing was ridiculous and that she was too, and that, whatever her mother's standing or intent, she must simply bring to the situation enough goodwill for two. She composed her features. Harbouring goodwill was another of the world's most impossible things to prove. She wished she might send her blood off for analysis where notice would come back that all was friendly and true. She tried out one or two sentences on the threshold. 'When I was a child I know you were under a lot of pressure and suffering yourself in some way I still don't understand and it was a bad time for you too and I absolutely forgive you and I just want us to have one conversation about it and then once it's out of the way let's never make mention of it again.'

'Why do you say "make mention"?' her mother might shoot right back. 'Why not simply "mention" on its own?' There would be a sharp little flash in her eyes as she picked her daughter up on this small failure of style. Forlorn suddenly, Harriet raised her hand

and knocked and pushed open the door. The room was empty, the patient gone.

In the corridor she called out too loudly for a nurse but no one came. Finally last night's cleaner ambled into view, dragging a mop with him and a small yellow plastic prop-up danger sign with an image of a skidding person on it.

'Where's my mother?' she cried.

A young student nurse appeared, dressed for theatre. 'A lady and gent collected her this morning,' Harriet was told. 'The doctor discharged her after breakfast.'

'You don't know where they were heading?'

'They might have left a message at reception.'

'There's no one there.'

'You wait here.' The voice was kind now, recognising 'a situation'. ('What is a situation?' Harriet asked her class when the word came up in a book she was reading them. 'Your mum and dad arguing, that's a situation,' Lucy said.) 'I'll go and find someone.'

'Thanks,' Harriet called.

Almost instantly she returned with an older woman.

'You're enquiring after Mrs Mansfield?'

'Yes I am.'

'And you are?'

'I'm her daughter, Harriet.'

'Oh. Mrs Mansfield's other relations came and collected her this morning' – she checked in a notebook that lay open on the desk – 'at ten twenty-seven.'

'And do you know where they took her?'

'Home, I believe.'

'To their home or her home, do you know?' Were they really, all three, to make the pilgrimage to Paris?

'I'm afraid I don't know,' the woman said. She was trying to be kind.

Harriet dialled her brother's number. 'Colin, it's Harriet.' She spoke the words mildly, without a hint of hurt. 'Any chance you could give me a ring please,' she said, 'when you have a moment, just to fill me in. Many thanks. Just wondering where Ma is and what I can do to help. Harriet here.' In this situation, she told herself, you have absolutely no rights. Well, she would fight for them.

In the corner of the lift, going down, Flora's mother and Sophie were clinging to each other wildly; you could feel moist heat emanating from their bodies locked in this passionate embrace. The smell of hair and sweat and skin throbbed in the rattling tin box. Fig body lotion? Apple shampoo? So consumed were they in this act of mutual comfort, or contrition, that they didn't even sense another person. Harriet blinked. Few things embarrassed her. She studied the sisters acutely, as a scientist might, she thought, and when the lift thudded to its ground-floor station she hopped out and scuttled off into the rain.

A year later, when Colin had finally agreed to meet her in a small designated chamber in the presence of a therapeutic mediator – it had been his condition for their meeting – they had sat in virtual silence for the best part of an hour. Finally Colin addressed the avid little room. 'You know, our parents should never have been allowed to have children.' There were echoes and echoes of regret in his voice.

Seagulls at the window made loud swooping noises and the sun brightened and brought everything in the room up to a blinding white. Harriet felt years of days and hours full of lonely dismay seep out of her, gathering starkly in the dazzling little room. The mediator person stood and went to the window and let loose the clattering slatted blind. Colin flinched and calmed himself visibly. It nearly did not matter that he said he still could not see her in his life. He regretted the feeling, perhaps, but it was a strong one and he thought it unwise to neglect it. You got into trouble that way, was what he said.

He wished his heart could go out to her more, his wife explained a week later in a letter on blue paper, and maybe one day, at some point . . . but not quite now. It wasn't safe, she was to understand.

Or if not understand, accept. Or if not accept, still heed his wish that he be left alone by her. It was still too raw, you see.

She did see. She understood everything. Something vast had been shared, it was what you might term a highly substantial crumb. But there was relief and triumph in knowing that in the face of his pain she had been quite magnificent. She had let him entirely off the hook of her.

'I'll do whatever you want.' She spoke quietly, nodding and smiling. She would stay away, she really would, if it meant his happiness. He would come round eventually. It wasn't a bearable option that this might not happen so she did not entertain the thought. 'People Always Come Round' was a chapter that she often wrote.

Colin could not even look at her. He had buried his long face in his chest and his crossed wrists made a cage over his head, and Harriet saw his right knee was shaking quite violently and she wished she had the confidence to take it in her arms.

As Long as You Like

The noticeboard had been requesting items for the Christmas Fayre since the start of term. Harriet had drawn, printed and hand-coloured posters with all the delights of the season: bulging stockings hanging from a carved mantel, a curvaceous Madonna and child, snowmen with raisin buttons and carrot noses and a snow-dusted Santa with more than a passing resemblance to Charles from the corner, a gaping sack spilling parcels at his boots. The proceeds would go to the night shelter at the end of the street. She saw its inmates shuffling out most mornings, bleary-eyed in the bright light, blinking at the fresh day stretching before them.

There was still no news from her brother or her mother; Harriet recollected this difficult fact every hour or two. She left further messages, short ones, long ones, in Paris, in Sussex. She even tried the hospital again. Her feelings on the subject came and went. Perhaps I might visit at the weekend, she consoled herself lightly. She put this suggestion in her next telephone messages and saw herself in striped nurse's uniform, proffering iridescent pink medicine no one wanted on a stunted plastic spoon. You don't even know which country they're in, she reminded herself drily. Of Lucy there was also no word. The point of everything seemed to be receding.

Only Honey gathered something was distressing her. 'Would you like me to help sort through the Christmas Fayre stuff with you after school? Can't wait to see what's in those bags in the hall.' It was an oddly intimate process, Harriet thought later, as they knelt to their task, not a million miles from going through a dead person's things.

'Hey, this looks interesting.' Honey unfurled a narrow pink ribbon rosette on a grey box to find a tissue-swathed underwear set, a lightly quilted lilac satin bra, low and plunging, with scales of turquoise lace. She giggled and thrust the box at Harriet. The matching briefs were highly scanty.

'What have we here?' Harriet asked in her most headmistressy tone.

'Oh my goodness, there's a card! Open it quick!' Honey urged, putting it into Harriet's hands.

Harriet slid the small rose-pink lozenge of paper out of its pink envelope. Her face lit with a smile. 'Till tonight!' Harriet bit her lip. 'Kiss kiss.'

'Tina will go insane when she sees these.'

'She might, she very well might! Would it be very corrupt to put them to one side for her?'

'So wrong, but so right!' Honey laughed.

'Honey, you don't have to be anywhere, do you? It's very kind of you to help with this.'

'It's fascinating. Shall I? Oh.' The next bag contained an assortment of old shoes. The smell of sour milk was overwhelming. 'In the bin with the lot?'

Harriet nodded.

The telephone rang abruptly but Harriet didn't move.

'Shall I get that?' Honey asked and stood up to answer. 'Hello?

Winchester House? Hello? Hello?' She replaced the receiver. 'No one there,' she said. The phone rang again instantly. 'Oh, hold on one moment please, I'll get her, she's right beside me. Oh. All right, are you sure? Yes, but she's just ... All right. Yes. I'll make sure she ... All *right*!'

As slowly as she could Harriet raised her head.

'It was your brother. He was ringing in haste, he said, so he just wanted to leave a message rather than actually—'

'Oh?'

'The message is ... um, what he said was, best not to come at the weekend.'

'Oh?'

'That was all really.'

'Did he say ... ?'

'He just said, his exact words' – Honey was trembling slightly – 'that it wouldn't work. No, "wouldn't quite work".'

'Surely that's up to my mother.' Harriet's voice was fierce.

Honey blinked. 'Of course it is.'

Harriet shook her head. She felt the further humiliation of water gathering at the sides of her eyes. Honey's entire body braced as she tried to absorb her employer's feelings. Harriet had seen Honey respond to the children's casual distress with this sort of concentrated care. She didn't know the history but she understood the strength. It was a split-second decision that needed to be made, several times a day in a nursery environment, to console or to distract.

Honey made her choice. Rummaging in a checked laundry bag she pulled out a pair of yellow duck slippers with eyes and beaks and webbed feet, inserted her hands in them and had one attack the other with a flurry of wild quacks. Harriet grabbed one of the slippers and cooed and bucked and quacked in response. Honey's duck was feminine and possibly broody; the noises were haughty and anxious. Harriet's duck was eager and less complicated, its quacks staccato and excitable. And after a minute or two their duck banter faded just as quickly as it had begun and the two women, without any sort of embarrassment, put the slippers to one side and resumed their adult talk.

'I'd like there to be lots of jams and preserves and pickles on the cake stall,' Harriet said. 'And shall we have the children making coconut ice and peppermint creams in boxes which can be bought as Christmas gifts?'

Honey nodded away with enthusiasm. 'Serena says her grandmother has an urn we can borrow if we can find somewhere safe to put it. We'll have to check with Linda. Health and safety.'

But something was slightly wrong. Harriet's eyes had tears that they just could not contain. Once again her mother was immaculately away. What, of good, had passed between them now seemed merely just another cruel— *Being Unbelievably Stupid* by Harriet Mansfield. *The Sequel.*

'I know it isn't right to ask you but I shouldn't telephone my brother, should I, to talk things through, do you think?'

'Well, you could, but ... '

'But? But you don't think?'

'Well, I suppose you could ask him why your visit doesn't work for this weekend, but ... '

'I might not like what he has to say.'

'But maybe I'm wrong, I don't know.'

'You don't think you could have misunderstood in some way?'

'It's not impossible but I don't really think it's very likely ... '

'You think it's clutching,' Harriet spoke the words very evenly, 'at straws.'

Honey nodded. 'I mean sometimes it helps to have it out, but ...'

Harriet nodded. 'I'm sorry to ask you impossible things. My family has this effect on me.'

'Everyone feels like that sometimes,' Honey said, then bit her lip.

Harriet gave a hollow laugh.

'Although, although the good thing is,' Honey weighed her words, it was almost as though she were composing a letter of condolence, 'the strong thing to hold on to maybe, is that you and your mother really enjoyed each other when she was ill. You came back so happy and full of her, how she had been and what she said and did. And I think that the fact that things were a bit lovely for a while, even if they aren't now, shows you that it was, that it is, possible.'

'Thank you very much, Honey,' Harriet said.

The telephone was ringing once more and Honey, with Harriet's permission, answered it briskly. She grabbed a pen, then discarded it and searched for another that wrote. 'Okay,' she said. 'Great,' she said and 'Thanks.' She put down the receiver. 'It was Tessa. Sounded quite upset. She says can you come to her flat. They're not at Lucy's place. I wrote down the address.'

'She wants me now, does she?'

'She's so fond of you,' Honey said. 'Lucy I mean. You have this extraordinary ability with the children. I've never seen anything like it. It's amazing. It's almost as though you actually—'

'Nonsense!' Harriet held up her hands in protest, but the skin on her forearms had reddened happily. 'And you mustn't speak like an obituary.'

'Here's the address. I know the street. I'll draw you a little map from the station. Something so funny happened today. Lily was playing with the dolls in the garden and she sat them both down and looked at them very seriously and arranged them, shuffling them round a bit and everything, and then she said, "Look, I'm afraid there's a bit of a crisis on and one of you is going to have to go to Nana's."'

'Oh no!' Harriet laughed for several seconds, then her smile straightened and dimmed. Is there not a single child at my school with a stable home life?

At the Underground, Harriet sat on an orange plastic seat and waited for the train's hushed roar. She began to catalogue the items gathered at her feet: a discarded magazine cover showing a naked woman both chesty and emaciated, a peach-coloured foam burger box leaking red sauce and a pinked ring of pickle. Next to this was a copy of the local paper, its pages marked with zigzag boot prints. She felt a faint rash prickle at her collarbone. She rose and peered at herself in the convex mirror at the end of the platform. She made the most dismissive gesture she knew.

Tessa's little flat was half the upper storey of a red-brick Edwardian house. Through a bay window Harriet saw a child in school uniform eke out chromatic scales on a Victorian upright piano. A high window opened and Tessa's head peeped out.

'If I throw you down the key can you let yourself in?'

Harriet picked her way up the creaky stair. 'Hello?' she called from the slip of hallway. 'Hello?'

Lucy ran out of a nearby unlit room, door slamming behind her, and hurled herself against Harriet's care.

'Hello there!' Harriet said. She took an awkward sideways step while Lucy clutched the space above her knees. It was a long time since she had known such a greeting. Lucy began to cry and her tears rained down on Harriet's shoes.

'Hi.' Tessa appeared. The two girls were dressed in identical pyjamas which were of pink flannel printed all over with light grey cats. Tessa had smoky rivulets of black kohl all down her face. You are the grown-ups now, Harriet whispered to herself.

'Now,' Harriet said, looking Tessa kindly in the eyes. 'Let me make you a cup of tea. You'll help me, won't you, Lucy?' She picked up the child and carried her into the kitchen and located the kettle. She found a tray and two mugs which she energetically rinsed. There was no milk. There was no tea.

Harriet brought a cup of hot water apologetically to Tessa in the bedroom, stepping gingerly over the carpet which was strewn with soiled clothing: tights, pastel-coloured balled-up knickers, bras, odd discarded packets of this and that, cotton buds, bits of tissue, sweet wrappers, crumpled magazines, a shampoo bottle, a plastic glass. She would not look too closely. A half-eaten cereal bar. Lucy was holding her by her skirts. 'Oh, I'll tell you what,' Harriet said. She took Lucy back into the kitchen, unpacked her bag and spread the phials of glitter and sheets of red and green and gold shiny paper on to the small white plastic table which was pushed against the wall. 'I thought we might make some Christmas decorations,' she put the words lightly. She quickly drew and cut out three small white cardboard angels. 'Shall we decorate these? I'm just going to check on Tessa for one second but if you could make a start, that would be—'

Tessa lay huddled on the bed, clutching a pillow in a flowery case.

'How are you?' Harriet said.

'She's buggered off.'

'The mother has? Without saying where?'

Tessa nodded.

'Did she say when she'd be coming back?'

She shook her head. 'Didn't even say she was going.'

At that point Lucy wandered in and climbed on to Tessa's belly. 'When's my mum coming back?'

'I'm not exactly sure, darling,' Tessa replied, as if it really were the oddest thing. 'I'll let you know as soon as I know. Soon, I'm sure!'

'Can I watch telly?'

'What do you think?' Tessa appealed to Harriet.

'I think a small amount of television now and then is fine,' she replied. 'A life that's too wholesome isn't . . .' but she couldn't think exactly what it wasn't.

A family of macabre, sugared-almond-coloured cartoon bears cavorted on to the screen and Lucy climbed down on to the carpet and settled herself at the foot of the bed. Tessa crept down beside her and Harriet sat on the floor at Tessa's side. We are three cheery shunned baggages, Harriet thought.

'She's been having these terrible nightmares,' Tessa whispered. 'Waking up screaming in the middle of the night.'

'I'm sure you need a break. Would you like me to stay here with Lucy while you have a lie down or go and see a friend for a couple of hours or a film or—'

Tessa gasped. 'Oh my God! Really? Are you sure?'

It almost didn't matter that her own mother had deserted her when there were other deserted people in need of her care.

'Of course. Let's see. It's six twenty now. Why don't you pop out right now?'

'She's not had supper—'

'Not to worry. We'll manage. As long as you're back by nine or so. Or ten. Ten thirty. Whatever suits. I'm sure you need a break. I'll pop back into the kitchen so you can get ready, shall I?'

Twenty minutes later Tessa emerged in a 1940s black crêpe dress and black polka-dotted tights. On her eyelids was the most delicate pearlised lilac shimmer. She was transformed into a starlet from old Hollywood.

'Oh!' Harriet said. 'You're magnificent. Do try to have a wonderful time.'

'Thanks.' Tessa shrugged. 'Kill or cure,' she murmured as she slipped out of the door.

Harriet moved herself on to the floor next to Lucy and took her hand.

'Are you all right?' she whispered but Lucy didn't answer, her eyes mesmerised by the pink and green dancing bears capering merrily towards ice-cream island.

Then, 'I'm hungry. But there's only the surreal.'

'The surreal?'

'You know, Rice Krispies.'

'Oh, yes!'

'But I think we finished them at lunchtime.'

'That's no disaster. Not at all. We could ... er ... we could go out to a café but you're all cosy in your pyjamas ...'

'We could phone up for a pizza!'

'Excellent. I've never done that before.'

'There's a thingy from a pizza place by the kettle.'

Harriet telephoned and placed an order for the family meal. It was unbelievably expensive but they were in a sort of low-level crisis.

'How thrilling! It will be here in twenty minutes!' she said. 'Can you last until then?'

'I don't know what to do any more,' Lucy said, after a while.

'Are you feeling very—?'

'He's got a new girlfriend. It's broken her heart.'

'Do you mean your father has?'

'No no no. Tessa.'

'Oh?'

'She's crying for him. I try to be good but ...'

'But?'

'She's going round to the place what he works in. He gives out the drinks.'

'Oh, I see.'

'She is crying for him in the night. He didn't tell her. He's wrecked up her life.' She began to cry again.

'Oh, I'm so sorry, Lucy. Poor Tess and poor you.' Just then the doorbell rang.

'The pizza man!' Lucy almost screamed. They both ran down and Harriet fed notes to the young lad who stood nervously next to his motorcycle. He handed them two white boxes and a bloated carrier bag.

Upstairs they spread their feast out on the little table. There were two giant pizzas, bloody-faced, the size of dartboards. A large foil package contained thick yellow rounds of garlic bread. There were chicken wings swathed in orange grease, a tub of coleslaw, a cup of spicy beans, two tins of fizzy orange and a large container of chocolate ice cream.

'Yay!' said Lucy. 'Everything's unhealthy!' She tore a giant triangle from her pizza and disposed of it swiftly, her lips and nose instant orange, her chin bearded with strings of cheese. She clawed the centre from a round of garlic bread. She picked up a chicken wing and bit into it, right through the bone. She took up a drumstick in her other hand. 'Do I look a bit like Henry VIII?' she said.

'Well, perhaps a teeny bit, but do be careful you don't get a tummy ache.' Harriet did not want to be headmistressy, fun-free.

Lucy had embarked on another pizza portion. Her technique was very streamlined and efficient. She scraped the flesh off a chicken wing with dazzling speed, added some beans and rolled it up into a parcel with some pizza dough, devouring the whole in four quick bites. Then she began again.

'Lucy,' Harriet tried again, 'how about a—'

Lucy interrupted her. 'I know, I know. I'll get fat. All anyone in the world cares is not getting fat.'

'Actually, I was going to say "How about a game of I Spy?"'

'Okay,' Lucy nodded, 'in a minute,' and put another wing in her mouth, savouring the flabby skin, spitting out the shards of bone and gristle. 'This is a delicious thing.' She spoke the words calmly and with happiness. 'Shall we have the ice cream now?'

'How about a nice refreshing bath?' Harriet asked when Lucy slowed between bites.

'Okay.' Lucy shrugged her shoulders and peeled off her pyjama top. She shook her head with hostility. 'Look at my enormous horrible tummy,' she said. 'Urrgh!'

'You are perfect,' Harriet said. She was.

The bath filled, and Harriet tested the temperature with her elbow, rounding up some empty shampoo bottles, an egg box and a plastic cup, carefully setting them afloat. She kept a distance from the naked child. Lucy climbed in and stretched herself out. Harriet sat on the floor on the landing opposite, legs crossed at the ankles, singing water songs, sea shanties, swimmers' ditties, pirates' tunes. Lucy joined her: '*And we jolly sailor boys were all up aloft, And the landlubbers lying down below below below, And the landlubbers lying down below.*'

'Why can I not have this?' Harriet thought.

After ten minutes Lucy climbed out and Harriet threw her a towel and the pyjamas she had been wearing earlier and requested that she dry herself. The situation, as it stood, was untenable, professionally, but that did not mean she should incur extra extravagant risks. When she was dressed Harriet re-entered the room.

'Have you got a bit of a tummy ache?' Harriet stroked the child's damp head.

'Only in a fun way. This is the best day ever!'

Lucy climbed into bed and Harriet brought in a plastic chair from the kitchen and sat beside her at the bed's lip. She read about a toy rabbit who wanted to be real. She read about a blacksmith's country wedding in a field of yellow corn. She read about a boisterous young man who terrorised his younger brother and a mouse who longed with all her heart for ballet school. Lucy asked interested questions at intervals. 'What's anvils? What's a *arabesque?*'

When Robin and Caroline were born Harriet had been allowed, at first, brief visits. Once she had even held Caroline for a quarter of an hour. Her head smelled very faintly of vanilla sugar. Her little toes. Her thumbs! She had sung 'Speed Bonny Boat' until the baby went to sleep in her arms.

'Can you do the Hi-Lo song?' Lucy was asking.

Harriet cleared her throat. *'A song of love is a sad song . . .'*

Within a minute Lucy was asleep. It was nine-eighteen. Harriet wrote down the time on a paper napkin branded with the logo of the pizza place. Tessa would be back soon. She drank her orange drink sitting at the bedside. Lucy's breaths were even and smooth. She had never put a child to bed before. It was the loveliest thing. She gazed at Lucy's soft scalp and stroked her wispy fringe. She shook her head and a knot of anger rose up in her. 'Please don't start,' she warned herself. She stood up and went to the window and opened it an inch or two.

She telephoned Honey. Honey was in a bar that was full, by the sound of it, of raucous women.

'It's nothing,' Harriet said. 'We'll speak tomorrow. All's well.'

'You're sure?'

'Quite sure, thank you.'

She stretched out on the floor beside the bed, parallel to the child but two and a half feet below, allowing herself to doze a little. Lucy's breaths were strong and calm like the sea's sounds. Her white-blonde hair glowed in the dimmed light. Harriet, half asleep, opened her eyes for a moment, glancing at the clock on the DVD machine. It was twenty past twelve.

She dialled Tessa's number but there was no answer. *I'd Like to Box Your Ears Young Lady* by Harriet Mansfield. She sat thinking and dozing until it was one o'clock. Tessa's young man, she supposed, had 'come through'. It was irresponsible, certainly, but she was a twenty-year-old girl, unhappy and in love, not somebody's middle-aged aunt.

She peered at Lucy in repose, her arms wide open as if to welcome the world. In the morning they would wash and dress and brush their hair, then take the Underground together in to school, stopping at the café on the corner for toast or eggs.

Just then Lucy sat bolt upright in bed, eyes closed, and started coughing terribly, a loose wet retching cough that could mean only one thing. Harriet ran into the kitchen and fetched the large plastic washing-up bowl from the sink and held it below the child's mouth. She was not looking forward to what would appear. The coughs lurched and Lucy's stomach beneath its pyjamas visibly stretched and then contracted. Her throat opened, a long low burp, and her mouth gaped – but nothing came. Lucy lowered her head down to the pillow. She slept on. The moment passed.

On the bedside table there was a shoebox filled with hair bobbles and ribbons, elastic rings, combs, two brushes, some headbands and tortoiseshell slides. Lucy's hair was long and silky and white blonde, with almost no trace of yellow. It would be all right to arrange the child's hair, would it, in the morning? Surely. She stood and picked up the box and fingered the hair ornaments. If it were plaited now, her hair, she would wake to a head full of ethereal waves. She stared at the child sleeping, her beautiful soft face against the pillow, peaceful, flushed, smiling, three toes peeping out from under the covers, in descending sizes. There was a slight gurgling noise. Lucy was laughing in her sleep.

Harriet stood and went into the bathroom and rinsed out Lucy's thin flowery dress and her pink socks and set them to dry over the towel rail. The clothes looked forlorn, evacuee-ish. She rubbed some toothpaste on to her teeth with her finger, splashed her face with water and smoothed down her hair. In the mirror for a second she saw her mother's hard Parisian eyes, but she shunted the image away. In the kitchen she cleared away the remainder of their crazy supper, tipping the gormless pizza into the lidless bin, rewrapping the wings in their foil and disposing of them too. Thick orange grease ran down her wrists and she scrubbed herself clean with the dish brush. Then the sound of the front door opening very slowly, and a soft guilty clicking as it closed. A few seconds later Tessa stood before her.

'I'm so, so, so sorry,' Tessa whispered, shifting her weight uneasily from one foot to the other.

'Don't worry too much about that. I did say be as long as you like, didn't I? How did it go?'

Tessa shook her head from side to side several times, then she flew into Harriet's arms and sobbed hotly and without a hint of caution against her employer's daughter's headmistress's chest.

Some time after Christmas, a little burned but not quite vanquished, Harriet tentatively rang the bell at the local night shelter. 'Hello?' she called into the frank spring air. 'Hello? Anybody there?'

The centre was loosely linked to the local church. There were six full-time staff and numerous unpaid helpers, some of whom were alumni of the centre and did not quite like to make the break. There were bars to all the windows and the entrance was made of reinforced aluminium.

It was ten past nine in the morning, just after they turned the residents out for the day. You could see the men clustered in local doorways, smoking cigarettes, eking out a bag of chips, wisps of vinegary steam and smoke mingling in the air with white breath. Six p.m. was opening-up time. Nine hours to fill with almost no cash was not a picnic. Harriet wore her worst skirt and her best jersey. She made efforts to tone down her voice. She was eager and clean.

'Morning. I wonder if you need any volunteers at the moment. I've got a few evenings a week free and one or two afternoons. I live just across the street.'

'Okay,' the woman said warmly. It was a good start.

'I have experience. I'm a hard worker. I can turn my hand to anything. I can cook. I can clean. I can sew. No job too big or too small. I am sounding like a plumber's van now,' she said.

The woman laughed. 'Tricia,' she said. 'You look familiar. I've seen you around. Didn't you used to work at that school up the street?'

'That's right.'

'I used to peer in through the windows sometimes when I was walking past on my breaks, see what you were getting up to.'

'Oh no!'

'One time everyone was singing and dancing in fancy dress and an old boy was playing the piano, and another time you were making dollies' clothes out of doilies and ribbons and a girl came in with a tray of jam tarts.'

'We did always have something lovely at three o'clock.'

'You could smell them in the street. I was tempted to join you.'

'You should have done!'

'But they closed the school, didn't they?'

'I closed it. I . . . It was doing quite well. But then my mother was ill and we became very close for the first time in my life which was something I had always wanted. And then she got better and she didn't want to know any more and it sounds mad to say so, but it kind of did me in. Silly I know, at my age! My deputy said she'd be happy to continue but I thought I'd take a bit of time to think things through. Get my strength back. I didn't want to be running things when I wasn't a hundred per cent. Not fair on the girls, somehow. I ought to have been able to shrug it all off, but . . . you know what it's like. You don't always bounce back as fast as you'd like. We weren't told to close down. It was nothing like that. Even the police said it wasn't our fault in the end.'

The Small Hours

The next morning, at school, a glut of prizes for the Christmas Fayre appeared including a suite of lime-green leather travel accessories, six engraved crystal tumblers, two virtually new beige bridesmaid dresses, a wicker picnic basket filled with brown and white plastic willow pattern china, and some boxed and unworn maroon leather cowboy boots with floral tooled uppers.

'People are *so* good,' Honey said with a questionable smile.

'Oh, the dears!' Harriet answered mischievously.

Lucy was nestled against Harriet's side. 'This is cosy,' she said.

During morning break while Honey and Linda took the girls round the garden on a mini beast hunt Harriet telephoned her brother. 'What news of Mother? Harriet.' Be stylish, be telegrammatic, she thought. After break, when the small clear containers swarming with ants and grubs had been catalogued and leaves had been gathered for the beasts' own lunch, Harriet led the girls upstairs for some work on the computer. At lunchtime she tried her brother again. She tried her mother. '*Je vous aide, madame?*' she heard herself say.

The following day at two o'clock Lucy's mother, Candida Meyer, came at Harriet humbly. Gone were the elaborate costumes, the skirts either ankle length or barely there, the astonishing boots, the fashion coats (or even capes) strewn with loops and studs and vents and straps and epaulettes. Instead she wore, well – how best to describe – the sort of get-up, prim blouse and skirt, that would inspire confidence in her maternal arts in any court in the land.

'I've been trying to get in touch with you. Which, I might add, has been a rather worrying experience,' Harriet began. 'We've left,' she glanced at a booklet of stapled papers relating to the case, indicating clearly that there *was* a pile of bound papers and there *was* a case, 'fourteen telephone messages for you, besides sending three emails and two letters. It doesn't look good. In fact, it isn't good.'

'I'm sorry if I've been hard to pin down,' the mother said. They took their seats opposite each other, squared as it were for their little battle. 'Here's the thing,' she began her *pitch*, was it? 'Firstly Paul and I have gone our separate ways. Which is fine. But he's left us, or rather me, with a load of debts. I've been in LA trying to get things organised. Anyway I'm glad to say the trip has really paid off.' The woman paused as if expecting congratulations, but even she saw it was a great deal to ask.

'Your daughter has been suffering, Ms Meyer.'

'Yeah, I do feel bad about that, but what else was I supposed to do?'

Something rebellious and ugly reared up in her tone but she quashed it effectively, Harriet thought. She was afraid, Harriet could see that now. Somehow she had detected in her daughter's headmistress some kind of power that could threaten to destabilise her.

'I know you've given both Lucy and Tessa a lot of support during this time and I'm so grateful.' She worked her lips into a smile. 'I bought you a little present to say thanks.'

Please God, Harriet thought, not some of your jewellery. She envisaged more pieces from the same line – *Willy* or perhaps *Wank* – but it was a small leather case filled with ten bottles for the bath, RELAX, LIGHT RELAX, DEEP RELAX, SUPPORT, RESCUE (EQUILIBRIUM), RESCUE (MUSCLE), REVIVE (MORNING) REVIVE (EVENING).

'Thank you very much,' Harriet said, bemused. Was it faintly insulting, this selection of tiny Alice-style cures that suggested she herself, at this particular time, was not perhaps all she ought to be? She decided, for the moment, to appear pleased. She'd give the . . . the offering to the Fayre. 'That's kind.' She put the box down. 'I'm not entirely sure what to advise in Lucy's case. She needs a long stretch of quiet, ordinary time with absolutely no comings and goings whatsoever in order to build up her strength. And Tessa needs a holiday. Is there anything you can do to reassure me you'll be more . . . more *about* over the next few months? We would absolutely hate, as a school, to have to take any sort of measures to . . . ' She stared at the woman harshly, she hoped, narrowing her eyes into their sternest glare. Another thought came to her. 'Will her father be planning to, d'you know?'

'I don't think he will, no. Maybe in time but right now . . . ' She dropped her voice and mouthed the word *Rehab*.

'Oh,' Harriet said.

'In Arizona.'

'Aha.'

'It's just something that happens.'

Harriet nodded. 'Thank you for being frank with me. May I be equally plain? I suppose what it boils down to, and I'm sure you'll agree, is that Lucy needs a better standard of care than she has been receiving. Is that something you ... ' She handed Candida Meyer the sorry document.

Page one: Wednesday noon, Lucy very upset, telephone call to mother at home, to mother's mobile phone and to mother's work, no replies. Call to nanny's mobile. Messages left. Nanny is asked at pick-up to ask mother to telephone. Email sent to mother at four o'clock also requesting phone call. No reply. Thursday morning, Lucy not herself again, telephone call to mother, text to mother's mobile phone. Nanny comes in and sits with Lucy for an hour, says she will ask mother to telephone. New message left on landline for mother. No reply from mother. Friday morning, Lucy not improved, postcard sent to mother requesting phone call and meeting. New email sent to new address found on mother's work website. Phone call to landline, phone call to work and mobile telephone, messages left. No replies. Telephone call to mother's sister – Lucy's emergency contact – no longer living at that address ...

Candida stood and took this little speech. She did nothing to indicate she would abide by these, what were they, *recommendations*, but she showed no objections. She didn't flounce, as Harriet feared she might if she went too far, clean out of the room, filled with rage. There were one or two sighs. The woman in her faux-humble garb sucked moodily on her bottom lip, her arrogant and selfish little head drooping towards the floor. Harriet had never felt so much like a headmistress in her life.

Just then the doorbell jangled loudly. 'Would you excuse me? I may just need to answer that.' Harriet rose to her feet. 'In fact I think we're finished here. I can show you out at the same time, perhaps?'

They took the stairs together. 'Goodbye,' Harriet said, not unkindly but with solemnity. So unfortunate to be named after a yeast infection, she thought. She drew back the door.

'Goodbye,' the woman murmured, but Harriet's eyes were glowing wildly now, her mouth a hoop of joy, for there in the middle of the street, at long last, was the gypsy wagonette in all its crimson glory flinging proud red shadows against the light stucco buildings all around. There was the bow top trimmed with cream, the scalloped edging with the original painted blue and white flowers, the four fully opening windows with cream slatted shutters and crisp dotted Swiss curtains fluttering from within.

'How d'you like her?' the delivery man called. Harriet beamed. 'Just wait till you see inside!' He threw back the stable door for her and lowered the five-rung steps. Harriet ducked her head and crept in, marvelling at the miniature home. Ingenious use had been made of the space, just as the brochure declared. There was a platform bed with red chequered quilt, a built-in padded bench with storage lockers underneath, an extending table, galleried shelving, a traditional wood-burning stove with narrow overmantel, a small wardrobe, part shelved, part hanging rail. Tears of pride softened Harriet's eyes.

She emerged to face Lucy's mother who was still standing on the doorstep. 'It's beautiful,' the parent conceded.

'Thank you, thank you,' Harriet said. 'That's good of you. The plan is to hire it out at weekends to film people. Pay for itself within the year.'

'But how on earth will you get it into the garden?' Candida asked.

Linda appeared. 'Crane's due in ten,' she smiled. 'If it's all right with you can I bring the girls out in threes to have a peek round?

We watched it arrive from upstairs. They're so excited.'

Honey came out on to the front step. 'I was thinking some of the girls might actually read their very first books sitting inside. Not that we encourage reading, of course, but some of them seem to be teaching themselves. Wouldn't that be just beyond great?'

Harriet nodded. 'It would be beyond great, yes,' she said.

At home-time, Flora's mother and her aunt appeared on the black and white tiles to collect her. Sophie was in high spirits, her rounded form encased in stunning red velour. She was snapping off lavender heads and throwing the flowers merrily into the air so they landed on her head like confetti. 'Helloa,' she called out to Harriet. 'Greetings! This must be your school. Can I come and live in the caravan?'

'It's just arrived. What do you think?'

'It's grand,' Sophie said. 'The girls can sneak inside when they need a fag!'

'Genius!' Harriet replied.

'Sophie's coming to live with us for a while.' Flora's mother was smiling.

'A change is as good as a rest,' Sophie said.

'We were all spending so much time at the hospital we thought she might as well decamp to the house.'

'Lovely,' Harriet commented blandly. Sophie traced wide circles with her foot against the chequered tile. 'At the weekend,' she confided, 'we're going to go ice skating!'

'Lucky things!' She was, Harriet thought, for all her impossibilities, one of the most charming people she had ever met.

'Flora not out yet?'

'I'll go and find her.'

Flora was sitting making an elephant's trunk out of shrimp-coloured sparkly play dough.

'Your mother's here, Flora.'

'Is anyone with her?'

'Your aunt Sophie has come to collect you too.'

'Tell them I'm busy, please.'

'It is home-time now. I can't very well turn them away.'

Flora sighed. '*All right,*' she shouted with notes of asperity Harriet was shocked to hear.

At six o'clock Harriet dialled her brother's number again. 'Only me!' She would have her opener humorous and spry. 'Just wondering how the patient's going along. Do give me a call when you have—' The words ran out. The telephone rang immediately. Harriet seized it but it was Sophie.

'Would you like to come to supper tonight?' she asked. 'We're having rack of lamb with rosemary potatoes and then lemon tart. Kitty's a very good cook. The lemon tart is bought, though. It looks a bit flabby to me. It's been dusted with icing sugar, the kind that doesn't melt in. How do they do that? But she's had the lamb marinating in a special sauce for ages. Coriander, I think she said. Mint? Limes? Oh yes, coriander leaves as well as the seeds. Did I tell you about my new leopard-skin washing-up gloves? Well, they're more like gauntlets really.'

'Lovely! I'd love to come,' Harriet sighed. 'What time would you like me?'

Sophie lit, before she answered this, a fresh cigarette. Harriet heard a sash window being shunted open. 'Afterwards we can do the washing up. I like making the things all sparkly. It's very satisfying. Come whenever you like. Bring your Marigolds!'

At seven fifteen, clutching a bottle of Pomerol, Harriet walked the nineteen yards along Winchester Crescent to Flora's house. She had changed into a fresh white shirt which had carefully ironed five-millimetre pin tucks running down the front. It was a dress shirt of her father's. She hoped the evening would be easy-going. Her desire for incomplete candour, just this once, was vast.

At the corner she paused to telephone her brother once again. Then she phoned her mother in Paris. Nothing came of either call. She must, for now and possibly always, forget. 'But when she was ill . . . she and I . . . ' Harriet protested wildly. 'You mustn't think that way. It's over. Finished. It was a freak thaw. I did try to warn you. She's got away.'

Outside Flora's house a tall tree boasted a mass of crisp fawn-coloured leaves. She broke off a short twig and scattered the brittle foliage. In the next door basement window an elderly woman on a stool at a table put down her book and began taking forkfuls of rice. Harriet breathed in the air deeply.

If they could only have seen, her family, the caravan hoisted by the crane over the rooftops, men on the slates guiding its progress, the vehicle glowing splendid in the light brown evening sky, then lowered with immense care into the back garden, set into place with the drawbar. It was one of the best things she had ever caused. She shook her head. I will not, she stated it quite clearly, she insisted upon it, have my morale destroyed.

She walked up the front steps to Flora's house and rang the bell. Her belief in herself would remain intact. After a while the mother answered.

'Oh! Hello there,' she said, cautiously. 'Would you like to come in? I'm afraid we're a bit all over the place. Sophie's giving Flora her bath and Miles is out for the evening and I'm supposed to be joining him in three-quarters of an hour. But we could have a quick drink in the kitchen.'

'No, no thank you,' Harriet said. 'It's fine. I just wanted to ask you if . . . ' Her mind was a complete blank.

'I know!' the woman said. 'I've got a bag of things for the fete here. I mentioned it earlier. Perhaps you'd like to—'

'I could take it with me now – that's really why I came.'

'So thoughtful.' The woman handed Harriet a plastic bag that was crammed with prosperous-looking items.

'I won't come in,' she said. 'I've rather a lot to see to this evening.'

'Well, if you're sure. It's all a bit fraught – I am sorry.'

'Not at all.'

She peered at an upstairs window and saw Sophie gazing down at her on the street, eyes wide and glaring. She was rubbing Flora's damp head with a blue facecloth. She made a sort of shooing motion with a flick of her wrist.

Harriet walked home, repeated the phone calls of the day and climbed into bed in all her clothes. She fell asleep and woke at midnight, rose and made herself a plate of bread and butter strips, eating them under the sheets. When they were gone she roused herself again and drew a photograph of her father in an oxblood leather frame from a high drawer. She remembered obliquely that when she was pretty small a conversation he had initiated about dispatching her to boarding school had been virtually stillborn. Was it her safety he was trying to ensure?

It was amazing, really, what people failed to know, what they couldn't bring themselves to see and the things from which they routinely shied away. Half-innocence was an endlessly appealing state. Every second of the day people all over the world rejected unsightly occurrences, because they were afraid of what they saw, scared to countenance the actions that their sightings would demand. It was perfectly natural and ordinary.

Harriet had sobbed at the boarding school suggestion. Why would they seek to punish her in this way? Her brother had already gone but he was ten and she was only six and a half. She wasn't that bad! She resolved instantly to be easier, better, more compliant, softer, more helpful. The matter was dropped almost straight away. Her father backed down, simply and calmly, taking himself out for the evening to some sort of function, leaving her mother vivid with rage.

She would try one more thing. It was a thought she'd first had some weeks ago. She would make a dignified suggestion for once in her life. She would telephone, no, she would send an email, it was one o'clock in the morning. She opened her computer.

Dear Colin, I trust all is well. Am assuming no news is good news on the mother front. Thanks for taking care of everything.

I've a new idea. On the 14th of next month, as you know, our father would have been eighty. This fact, at the very least, I feel calls for some fruit cake and a glass of champagne.

Will you and Ma and Maggie and the children join me at a location of your choice? My treat!

All my best, Harriet x

Three minutes later a reply.

You will excuse me, Harriet, if I decline the invitation to your festive gathering on the 14th of next month. It was, of course, more than thirty years ago, but I cannot bring myself to commemorate the life of a man who interfered with me.

Regards, Colin

Ten seconds later: Forgive my outburst of a minute ago. Am drunk and these are very trying times.

Then another email whose subject box said Please delete immediately without opening all emails I have sent today. Risk of grave virus.

Another email came whose subject was Delete all emails from C Mansfield instantly.

Harriet sat back in her chair, her hands shaking, her knees jerking wildly. It was a dreadful sense of excitement that she felt.

I am so shocked, Colin. So shocked and so sorry. What the devil – she deleted the word devil and changed it to fuck – did our parents mean by having children?

No reply.

Do you hate him? May I hate him on your behalf? For a second she had wondered about writing h8 as teenagers did. Where had that come from?

And then on her screen: Do you hate her?

He remembered! He remembered!

Did she know? Did he? May I telephone you now?

No, please don't ring. I'm not going to go into all that now. I need my bed. I drank masses of whisky this evening for some unknown reason. Not had a drink in more than a year.

I'm glad you did.

Better not make a habit of it. Maggie will kill me.

She'll understand this once. She knows, I presume.

She's been tremendous, yes.

And Ma?

I have attempted to raise the matter once or twice, in the last few years, but I don't think she can really quite hear me ... but I have sometimes thought she has always known.

She is a funny old fish.

Quite.

Then:

Harriet, please listen to me carefully. I am going to ask that you never ever refer to what I have told you. I can't speak about it. You're going to have to forget it. Give me your word please that you'll respect my wishes completely. I want you to banish it from your mind. You must never ever mention it not to anyone else and especially not to me. Do you understand? Can you promise me please that you'll do as I ask?

Sometimes in life you were evil unless you did exactly what was wanted. She shook her head. It was the same old story. The keys were cruel, or she was, as she struck them, almost apologising for her roughness as she typed.

I promise.

She waited a further ten minutes, but nothing came back. She pondered the suitability of a final, wry closing line such as: **They say, don't they, that it happens in all the best families,** but thought better of it.

Harriet did not want to sleep. She was afraid to dream. She went downstairs and wrote out some ideas for a nativity play, then reorganised the art materials into spotless rainbow ranks until it was dawn.

St Patrick's Day at the shelter! Harriet arrived at ten to six with a steaming vat of Irish stew. She had thirty paper hats with gold shamrock motifs hidden deep in her bag, in case they seemed childish and ignoble. She would ask Trish for advice about that. She did not know yet how things were done, but she wore her green jersey very frankly. Where was the harm?

She was popular with the men who used the shelter. They called her babe and sweetheart sometimes. 'In another life,' one man in his late eighties said, 'I'm sure I knew you. Did you grow up round here?'

'In Sussex,' she said.

'Miss the country, do you?'

'I hated it!'

'You remind me of my auntie Mary, my mum's older sister,' one of the younger men had said. 'Only she was four foot nine!' He cackled wildly. 'What's the weather like up there?'

'Haven't heard that before,' she said. Actually, she hadn't.

'This stew's half decent. Looks like shite but it tastes good.'

'Too kind!'

'You're a very good listener,' Trish told her.

'Ginger cake for pudding tonight,' she said. She'd made it with crystallised ginger in a large rectangular roasting tin.

'What no custard?'

'I'll bring some next time. There's whipped cream.'

'What about my cholesterol?'

'Well, I can nip out and get you some yoghurt if that would hit the spot.'

'You have the patience of a saint, do you know that?'

'Me? Oh no. I'm just enjoying myself, that's all.'

'What's your husband think of you spending your evenings with us?'

'Oh, he's very quiet on that subject. Pretty silent about everything in fact.'

'Invisible man is he?'

'One could say that.'

'Give us a cuddle.'

'Tempting as your lovely suggestion is, sadly I'm not allowed any perks with this job.'

'How many kids you got?'

She shook her head.

'What, none?'

'You *are* interested in my arrangements this evening.'

'No kids? No family?'

'I am a single person family.' She tried to speak the words with pride.

'This life is a pile of shite, isn't it?'

'Well, there is some truth in what you say ... but you've got to admit some of it's all right. Good bits come round now and then. I mean, this is lovely now ... '

'You are a soppy cow.'

'Guilty as charged.'

'Want some cake? It's not bad.'

'Oh no. I had loads of the mixture from the bowl. That's always when it's at its best in my opinion.'

'Lick the spoon, did you? You're such a big kid.'

'I know. I think it's what gives me my mad charm.'

Mornings Worse Than This

In the morning, while Serena and Honey took the girls for Grandmother's Footsteps in the garden, Harriet, unslept in last night's sorry clothing, frantically unpacked a large box that had just arrived.

What are you even doing? she asked herself, piling up red and pink melamine dishes in a meaningless tower in front of her, arranging the large scalloped oval platters, the little tea plates, the three-tiered pedestal cake stand. Her head was a complete nothing. I am doing, she replied, my best.

'No,' she said out loud. Not thinking, not feeling. You don't need, for life to continue, to do that all the time.

Just then the screech of brakes right outside the front door. Colin! She ran out into the street. She smoothed down her skirt and sent a hand up to her hair.

There was, of course, no Colin. She knew that. Only a lone squad car parked across the middle of the road and inside it a policeman talking animatedly into his radio. Harriet ran over to him and tapped on his window. He barely registered her but then another car drew up and seconds later the ordinarily quiet road smarted with shrill sirens. Front doors were flung open up and down the street. What was it? A small crowd began to gather: a woman leaning on the staunch navy hood of her pram stood by, mouth gaping, her hand pointing into the air; two red-haired schoolboys stopped abruptly, marks of horror in their eyes; the smirks on a pair of teenage girls, madcap with truanters' victory, fell sharply. On a doorstep a male author who worked from home, ashen and stricken-looking at the best of times, stood in stale shirt-sleeves with a mug of coffee, peering up at the sky. A cleaning woman in a sticky green apron and slippers ceased wiping down the bevelled glass panels of a front door and dropped her rag to the ground. A fire engine turned the corner sharply and parked right across the middle of the road, closing things off, like a punctuation mark.

The air darkened visibly. Harriet looked up. On her roof was a little child. It was Flora! She was standing determined by the building's edge, her toes peeping over the sheer wall, her face held high but turned away from the street. She looked like a ghost, her arms and legs out of focus and provisional in the heavy morning light. She clutched her little cherry smock to her sides. It would be cold up there. A flash of her face as she turned, the features hardened in eerie resolve. Another squad car arrived and another and an ambulance. Men spilled into the street, men in bleached coats, men in black uniforms, men in blue. On the roof the child folded her arms; she was observing the proceedings from her vantage point with a sort of cool intrigue. On the ground a sense of panic was rising, the air thick and swollen with fear. Men from the fruit market arrived to see what was occurring, their pockets, their faded half-aprons, jangling loudly with change. Some of the local shops and pubs had emptied. There were forty or fifty people standing now, all heads tipped back, all eyes fixed on the roof. Two policemen were stretching thick striped emergency tape over the entrance to the street to prevent any further traffic. Harriet made her way to the front where the retching sound of more tape unfurling sounded violently in the air.

'I am the headmistress of this school, the owner and proprietor of the building. I must go back in immediately. I'm very close to the child. I may be able to help. This is private property. Kindly move out of my way!'

'We're not letting anyone else in, miss,' the uniformed officer said. 'I'm sorry. We're confident we can turn the situation round; we have a trained negotiator. I'm sorry but you have to play it our way.'

A trained negotiator! Harriet spat the words, but she could see it was no use to fight. How had Flora got up there? No child had ever penetrated Harriet's private apartment before, let alone climbed the narrow wooden ladder where a small white trapdoor opened on to the flat roof.

Her sore heart swelled. Everything was slipping away. The men who had operated the crane for the caravan had come up on to the roof, first to assess the job, and one had remained on the phone to his colleague at the controls throughout, guiding the vehicle over its obstacles, the satellite dishes and the stacked chimney pots. 'Easy does it. Left a bit now, whoa! Down you come.' Harriet had expressly bid them to lock up after themselves, explaining the key's odd insistence on being pushed and lifted and squeezed to the right before the bolt would properly throw. They had, in fact, asked her to repeat this information twice. Despite this, the communal door between Harriet's apartment and the school must have been left open, the entry to the roof unlocked. It was monstrous. Why had she not checked? Unless the child had taken hold of the keys, wandered through her apartments, climbed the small white steps and launched herself on to the top of the building. Yet how had she managed to detach herself from Honey and Linda? From Tina and Serena? Harriet could not think. It was impossible that not one of her staff would have prevented her from straying. Could she really have loosed herself from their tight circles of care and wandered off?

But, wait a minute, she was forgetting the most important thing! The mother had phoned that morning, anxious and stuttering, to say that Flora would not be at school today. She had taken the call herself. She had been marked absent in the register. They had all had an awful night, was what the mother had said, and they were keeping Flora at home to sleep in. She must have set out on this journey from her own house, through her own attic, picking her way across the roofs to the roof of the school.

Harriet looked up again at the child whose slight body stood swaying in the light winds. She was all wrong there, the scale of her against the chimney stacks. Even the inky slates looked bogus, theatrical. The surroundings no longer made sense, the sky too blue for reality, the cherry smock too fiercely red. Flora's eyes were fixed to the ground. Was she marking out a spot on which to land? Harriet held her breath. She wept silently for Flora. It was such an adult form of protest.

A child who jumped forty foot on to the pavement would die unless caught. The police and ambulance men and the fire brigade were milling round the school entrance. It was like an incompetent military scene. They were sending the youngest, blondest policewoman up on to the roof now, briefing her, filling a string bag for her with toys and sweets. She clutched a child's red coat. The pain in Harriet's heart was of such a magnitude that she thought it might explode. 'She likes stories about horses,' Harriet called out. 'She likes ginger snaps.' She heard soaring piano music coming from a neighbouring house, suddenly, a record blaring from the attic floor.

Eight of the uniformed men on the street were unfurling an enormous round blue sheet with which to break the child's fall. Inmates from the shelter were offering their help to the officers. The mother arrived, merely passing with her shopping – new shoes from Old Bond Street – took in what was going on and screeched, 'Get her fucking down!' There was a flurry from the crowd as the mother began wailing hysterically. A policeman approached her and she buckled against him abruptly. He ushered her quite roughly into a panda car. The crowd gasped as the mother's behaviour seemed to strike the child with alarm and she moved slowly, in small sideways steps, along the building's edge, her body lurching forward, weight-lessly. Any second now she is going to fall, Harriet gave herself the warning, even if she doesn't mean to. Was there a corner of the blanket she might, herself, be allowed to take?

Instead she surveyed the mother's silent screams through the windscreen of the squad car. Her arms were flailing above the dash-board and all the colour had gone from her face. She vomited on to her coat, covering her mouth with her hands, but you could see the sick dripping thickly through her fingers. The policewoman sitting next to her dabbed at her with tissues and fed a comforting arm round her back but she flinched violently. Harriet looked away.

What the atmosphere was like in the school Harriet could not imagine. Were Tina and Serena, steeled or oblivious, still occupy-ing half the children in the garden with Greek myths? Had Honey and Linda begun the lino cutting in the art room above?

On the roof the policewoman was visible now six or seven feet away from the child. The men holding the blanket repositioned themselves slightly, obeying their senior officer's orders. They looked strong and, besides, the child could not have weighed more than three stone. Flora accepted the coat from the woman who promptly sat down on the floor of the roof and disappeared from view. 'She's reading a story now,' one of the officers announced. After one or two minutes the child wandered over to where she was sitting, to look at the pictures possibly or the better to hear. Then she sat down on the roof so that neither of them was visible. The crowd was silent, as though straining to follow the story themselves.

'What now?' Harriet glimpsed one of the large ambulance men mouth the words to his colleague.

'We wait,' came the reply. Harriet's eyes turned to the police car, where she could see the mother's hysteria mounting, her helplessness and anger, but moments later the female police officer emerged through the front door of the school, carrying the child like a trophy. The mother sprang forward and the child transferred allegiances, flinging herself at her mother's chest which was thick with heavy gold chains and flecked with milky vomit, lacing her arms round her mother's neck. The mother was livid, her face so dark and creased with fury that she did not allow herself to speak.

'Who's in charge of this ... this ... *school*?' You could almost taste the disgust in the senior officer's breath. He might as well have said 'so-called school'. A young policeman was interviewing everyone at the scene, making jottings with a pencil in a notebook. His colleague's face was broad with acne scars that gave his skin the appearance of terrain. 'I say we go inside, phone all the parents and evacuate the building. No one touch anything. I'm treating this property, until further notice, as a crime scene. Understand? Where's that red-haired woman who was fussing around earlier? The tall one? I need to speak to her.'

A young, wiry man with a long-lensed camera appeared and

starting taking photographs of the house. 'Is it true,' she heard him ask, 'that she employs alcoholic street people to teach the little girls?'

Harriet, in terror, buried herself in the bushes of the neighbouring garden, crouching down between some vicious bracken and the rubbish bins. There were times when you wanted to creep into hiding, like an animal. It was where Charles sometimes slept and there was a checked laundry bag with blankets and cushions in it and a paisley wash bag and a mug with an ivory-handled shaving brush and some folded shirts wrapped in polythene. She lay down and put everything she could grasp over her head.

Flora's mother was appealing to the senior officer, with her hands and arms pawing his pristine uniform, grabbing his elbow and shaking as she clasped him. He was moderately sympathetic. 'It's not her fault. Not the school's,' she protested, her voice childlike and shrill. 'Flora wasn't at school today. We live five doors down. She got up on to our roof at home and wandered across the roofs down the crescent to the school. She wasn't even at school today. She had a bad night so I kept her in. My sister's very ill. They were playing on the roof together last night ... it's just one of those things.'

In Charles's little lair empty wine bottles had been lined up, all ready to go to the recycling bins. There was quite an array. Harriet slumped for a few more seconds, then she roused herself. She must try to be— On a postcard taped to the bricks by his pillow she read, half in a dream:

Early rain
And the pavement's glistening
All Park Lane

In a shimmering gown.
Nothing could ever break or harm
The charm of London Town.

The police presence was gradually fading. Dimly she could hear the senior officer being assured by his negotiator lady that all the doors she had met with on her journey to the roof were firmly secured. She herself, she said as if to close the matter, had borrowed keys from a young blonde teacher and opened, with no small difficulty, the door to the upstairs flat, then the small aperture that led to the roof. There was no possibility that the child had got up that way through locked doors.

Harriet took this as her cue to re-enter the school. The police no longer stood in her way. She asked Honey and Linda, Tina and Serena to bring their groups down into the basement kitchen where they all sang Christmas carols while munching on strawberry ice-cream cones. It was only an hour until lunch but desperate measures were called for. School must end early that day. All the staff agreed. Local parents must hear about what had taken place first hand and as quickly as possible. Honey telephoned all the names on the school list and requested that the children were collected straight away because of a 'small problem with the building'. As each group of parents arrived Harriet ushered them into the ground-floor office, where Linda was typing up the newsletter in the corner, and explained what had happened in the calmest and lightest way.

The parents were harsh, some of them. 'There's a history of trouble in that family, isn't there?' one mother snapped. Was it wise to have accepted such a child as a pupil? One or two others took fright for their own children and asked to speak to a member of the police to verify Harriet's version of events. Harriet passed on the duty sergeant's telephone number. One or two of the younger mothers, impossibly sanguine, joked in good, solid cheer. 'All this proves is that your school is so popular,' they put it to her, 'that your children cannot bear to stay away, even when they are not well!'

Over the next hour Harriet watched the sad succession of pairs or straggly threes wandering down the street, some exhilarated by the prospect of an unexpected holiday, others made anxious by the scent of catastrophe that still hung in the crescent's air. Finally the staff left the building also. Honey and Tina, Linda and Serena, made their way into a local pub, stunned, their faces drained, their elbows linked tightly, and for once they had no chatter at all. Harriet had handed Honey a cluster of banknotes. 'Could you make sure everyone has a good lunch,' she requested. 'Or at least something good to drink. It's important after a shock like this.' Honey had smiled and squeezed her hand.

The building empty now, Harriet did not know how to proceed. The picture of that stick-like child teetering on the rooftop smashed at her heart: the wash of anguish on her serious face, the deep marks of woe. It was the worst thing she had ever seen, the toes poking over the side of the building, all primed for descent, the look of res-ignation on that strained face, the summoning of the will to action, the luminous sparks of adrenalin, that awful self-propelling urging instinct rising in one so very young almost impossible to bear. Harriet's head ached with the old, violent pounding. She wished she were back once again in the dank and gloomy space which Charles inhabited. His things were so lovely, the bone-handled brush, the neatly folded shirts with the frayed cuffs.

Flora's face was flashing at her: the high sorrow and hopelessness.

Harriet could not remain in the school alone. She slipped out of the front door and ran as fast as she could to the top of the crescent. She looked out across the grey and white noon that rose to meet her and drew her telephone out of her bag. Dialling quickly her brother's number she made a final, ruinous plea into his message service. 'Please Colin, I am so so upset. I don't know what to do. I know I am not allowed to ask you anything but the things that are going through my head. Could we just speak for five minutes. I can't manage it on my own. I'm so sorry but I need your help with this. Please please please can you ring.' She dialled her mother's long Parisian digits. 'Ma, it's Harriet here,' she said into the phone but it was still ringing. There wasn't any answer. 'Hello? Hello?' She heard a voice. 'I'm sorry to bother you like this. I'm just ... and something awful's happened, but— Hello?' and then she realised it was the answering machine after all, only the message had been changed, and her voice broke and she felt her body buckle with tears. 'I can't go on if you don't love me,' she said, but the words were flooded with mucus and her own disgusting liquid low morale. 'Please? I thought it didn't matter but I don't know what else to do.' The words were soft, desperate, almost a prayer.

'I don't know where you get your ideas from,' her mother would say. 'Are you having some sort of midlife crisis? Let's let each other off the hook, shall we? Call it stalemate. I'd like to resign and I know you would. The school was an inspired idea. Give yourself over to it. It's your vocation, like that woman in the book, the Brussels one. I'm getting old now and old people are selfish. Surely you can see that? You're a grown-up woman yourself. Do try, dear, to stop living in the past. That's my advice. Heaven knows, I haven't got what you want! You're an attractive woman, intelligent and determined. Don't waste your energy worrying about me! I like my life. Grandchildren are fun. Try putting me to the back of your mind. But all these great swags of emotion you cart around. You are funny! Where *do* you get it from? Not me. Certainly not your father!'

The fear of the crash, the crash itself, the illness lived out in endless, numbed days, then, if she were very lucky, the extended agonising convalescence period and then months later, with hard work and bravery, there you were again back at square one with all your nerve endings on the wrong side of your skin. Could she really do it all again? When you knew what was involved, scoop yourself out of your own dregs again? People said humans had no memory for pain, but she could remember it distinctly. The paths were still furrowed, ready for when it came again: she could recall its pointed sensations in an instant – their dark allure – and death lurking everywhere at the centre as well as the fringes of things, in your heart and mind and even in your joints. Only despair and nothing light or funny or clear or true for weeks on end, for months of hours. There was nothing she feared as she feared a return to that state.

How could you thrive when the people you loved wouldn't even—? It was a sort of disease that she had. Her head ached so badly she feared she was growing herself a tumour out of hurt, out of spite. They thought, her family, that they had quietly walked away, and with dignity, but really they could not have attacked her more if they had set at her with swords. The weight of neglect, of distaste, of disinclination even, it stole the life out of her. She had huge peaks, when she managed to get some sort of rise out of herself, but she couldn't sustain anything for long because the old disappointments always always returned. You could never escape for long. She knew that now. If the failure was entirely hers, a failure of detachment, of spirit and of character, then she fully accepted the blame.

She walked back to the house and saw that the last trace of police tape had finally gone from the surroundings and the front door gaped open. She led herself in and made her way up to her bedroom. She lay down on the floor, the huge unlovely bundle of her, her legs flinching at their own length, her shins pale, cracked and freckly, the scratch marks from the bracken which had cradled her arms so mercilessly, in the neighbour's garden, glowing red. The shame that riddled her person inflamed her heart and the room echoed with her brutal, convulsive sobs. She felt murderous and utterly vanquished. Sometimes you had to make a clear end of things. She could not be happy, she could not exist while they would not love her. She was a success, she knew, at false cheer, but what did that mean? She had made up her mind, so many times, that her morale wouldn't crack, but ... She had to accept first, fully, that she had lost. She did accept it, she did! The victory was all theirs, about that there was no doubt. She took a black comb from her bag and ran it through her hair with an automatic hand. She saw herself languishing in a minuscule cell. Then she drew a large bottle of supermarket headache pills from her bag. There was nothing of herself left to express. It was a warped philosophy, even she knew, but she started cramming handfuls of pills into her mouth and washing them down with cold tea. Four handfuls then five. She thought of her brother. She thought, separately, of her father. You had to keep them apart.

She ran out again into the street and cast her eyes about the damp and callous brick that met her eyes. She thought of her staff in the pub, of laying herself on their hands, but they must not see her in this state. They deserved better than that. Instead, she flagged down a taxi and asked the driver to take her the one and a half miles to the red-brick mansion block where Miss McGee had worked and lived last time they had met. There was no traffic. The branches of a large tree were pointing at her like fingers. Out of the taxi window everything was particularly still, as though it were dead.

She spilled out on to the pavement, handing her wallet to the driver. She was afraid the slanting houses might fall on her head. An estate agent's hoarding attached to the doorway announced that in this building there were two flats for sale. Harriet's heart soared. She shouldered open the heavy glass door and raced up the four flights to the landing she had not seen for almost two years. She cried out in a paroxysm of love and darkness at the familiar colourless carpet, neither ailing nor luxurious but exactly in between, the heavy brass door furniture, the front door that was peeling slightly, no more nor less now than the last time. She was muddied, she regretted it now and more than she could say, from her stint in the garden bushes; her dress was torn and her face was rubbishy with tears. She lingered at the threshold, unsure how to— her head a complete nothing. In the attic of her mind, long put away with other broken-down bits and things she'd laboured hard to forget, a figure emerged, lean and pale, her palms opened out towards Harriet's agonised pleas.

Are you real, Miss McGee? For one terrible second she wondered if she had made the woman up out of a huge, pressing need.

She rang on the bell, one short shrill sound, then fell to the ground on her shins. Miss McGee might have moved house, she might be dead. She might be with someone else. Another patient! She waited. There was A and E at the hospital, *her* hospital, she put it to herself mildly as she felt her head droop and her arms begin to numb. Miss McGee wasn't there. She staggered to her feet and sounded the bell again. And again and again.

Was that a stirring she heard, a slight sound? A dim light bloomed in the hallway. Harriet clutched herself with freakish glee. Footsteps came and with them the figure of a woman in dark clothing. What would she say? What would she seem?

Harriet had never done anything so unorthodox in her life. She recoiled from herself. What a position to put another in, another person whom you loved, who had loved you more practically and with more efficacy than anyone you had ever . . .

Pull yourself together. Harriet issued the command sternly. Present, she urged herself, a reasonable front.

The door opened and Miss McGee, in the flesh, gazed at her, with that mildly questioning air that had characterised all their hellos, all their goodbyes.

'I'm sorry!' Harriet bundled herself roughly against the door jamb. 'I know this is not what I'm supposed to do, but I didn't know where else to – I don't know what I've done but it's something terrible. Can you? Do you think you might be able to?'

She saw her predicament strike at Miss McGee's heart.

'Of course I can,' Miss McGee replied softly. Her strong arm guided Harriet into the hallway, without quite touching her skin. A half-eaten bowl of tomato soup, Harriet saw, perched precariously on the edge of a table, an undistinguished bread roll. There were tiny orange soup marks at the edges of Miss McGee's lips.

'Is it all right? Are you with someone, or—?'

'No no, it's a good time.' Miss McGee ushered her along the familiar corridor towards the room in which they had always had their talks, but there was not the usual smoothness in her movements. Something was seriously wrong; her face was contoured with something Harriet had not seen in it before. Her shoulders had stiffened. Was it age? Had something substantial gone wrong?

Harriet hovered and closed her eyes. When she opened them the familiar room looked hazy and there were thin slits of light dancing in front of her. The floor disconcerted her; ridged and cratered, it caught her out as she placed her footfalls, rising to meet her steps or sinking sharply away. There was all the same furniture exactly. She put out a hand to steady herself. There was her little chair! She had almost reached it.

'Do sit down, please,' Miss McGee's voice was saying. 'Are you able to sit down? Harriet?' she asked again. Perhaps she had said it many times. Then Miss McGee herself stood and draped over her shoulders a dark garment, picking up a large brown shoulder bag.

'Come with me,' she said. Her voice was so strange, the timbre of it ragged and at sea, but the words were clear. 'I think we need to go round the corner for a check-up. There's rather a nice doctor there in A and E, I've known him for years. With any luck he'll be on this afternoon. He'll take good care of you.' Her breathing had quickened slightly and Harriet felt the pressure of her grasp. 'It's going to be all right.' Miss McGee was talking non-stop. 'It's all going to be all right. Not to worry. That's it – lean on my arm. That's right. That's the ticket.' They muddled down the stone stairs as though joined at their limbs, Harriet stumbling at the bottom when the steps ran out. There were weights on her legs and she could barely lift them.

'Nearly there.' Miss McGee's voice was firm. 'Do you see they've opened a new patisserie? The bank's gone now, of course. But the butcher clings on. He certainly knows how to charge. They do mutton now and game and if you give them notice they'll order in special lines: venison or hare or what have you. Suckling pig, they claim, although I'm not at all sure that there's much call for that in these parts ... They've some sort of link with a large estate in Kent.

The newsagent isn't much changed. They have a DVD rental service now, I believe, but for how long? Do you see the pigeons up there on the top of the clock tower? They appear to be holding some sort of meeting!'

The street was thick with the oddest colours and scents. Harriet sagged and buckled in the older woman's arms. She put her hands over her eyes. I don't want anyone to see me because I'm dying, she thought. Miss McGee's clutch was tighter than ever. The knock of a pedestrian propelled Harriet towards the kerb's edge but Miss McGee hauled her back. She felt as though she were on strings. There was a zebra crossing that seemed to go on for miles. 'You're doing well.' Miss McGee kept up the chatter. 'In a few months this will just seem like another rotten joke. Not to worry. We're here now.'

There were pale steps which they mounted at some speed, and then a man and a woman, and her old friend the rusty lift and lights and all sorts of mysterious sounds. A nurse in royal blue was prodding her eyes and taking off Harriet's clothes. There was white piping on her cuffs. It wasn't cold, though. They fed her arms into fresh clothes, tied her up at the back, stepped her legs into paper knickers. The nurse washed her hands at a corner basin and rubbed in some pink liquid that smelled of gin. They were attaching her to some sort of apparatus now. Her arms were soft, her head flopped hotly against her chest. Some children walked into the room by mistake and went out again. One of them smiled the most beautiful smile.

'Did you see that?' Harriet spoke dimly through some sort of watery fog. 'Did you see that girl?'

Miss McGee was stroking her back, up and down, up and down. For a split second Harriet thought, am I going to have a baby? But she knew it wasn't that. It never was that. She blushed at her own stupidity. 'Is it all right?' she asked, softly. 'Do you think? Can you tell?' They were fixing a wire to her, making a small incision in the skin on her wrist. Tape was being taped by a young man. The lights were low.

'There's plenty of time,' Miss McGee said. 'You did the best thing in coming to me. Thank you for doing that.'

'Is it Josephine, your Christian name?' Harriet murmured.

'Geraldine,' Miss McGee said. 'Geraldine Charlotte.'

'Oh yes, I remember now.'

Miss McGee smiled briefly.

'This is all very much against the rules, isn't it?'

'Well,' Miss McGee said. 'Well, it seems to me we needn't concern ourselves with that unduly.'

Harriet closed her eyes.

'Keep her talking, please,' the man instructed.

'And what happens next, do you think?' Harriet asked.

'You're not to worry about that,' Miss McGee said. 'You're in good hands and I think you're—' She stopped and appeared to change her mind. 'I think,' she added, 'I think – and they are awfully good here – it's almost definitely going to be fine.'

'Keep her talking please,' the man repeated. A woman had wheeled in some sort of evil-looking machine. 'Keep talking. You must keep talking.' Miss McGee picked up a local newspaper and started reading to her patient a list of neighbourhood restaurants which had been reprimanded for hygiene infractions. A mouse had taken up residence in a canal-side pizzeria, a brown one, nine inches long. 'Squeak squeak,' the doctor said.

'Do you like Italian food?' somebody asked.

'Oh yes,' Harriet said. 'Very much. I ordered a pizza once and it was as big as a roundabout!' Everyone giggled. In a curry house near the station a fox had been found in the kitchen. 'Goodness gracious,' one of the nurses said in an Irish voice. Miss McGee had started up something new about what was it ... decorating ... housework ... gardens ... a holiday villa some friends were thinking of purchasing somewhere strange. Gibraltar perhaps. Malta. The Maldives. Have you been there, Harriet? Where was your last holiday? The lights were very very low. Miss McGee was holding her and pressing into her palms thick bolts of human warmth. Harriet smiled faintly. What she really wanted was to laugh but there was no feeling in her mouth.

You were bad in life to get what you wanted through such means, but no one was cross with her. She could not begin to think about people. If that's inhuman perhaps that's what I am, she thought. And it seemed to Harriet, quite vaguely then, that her mother and her father were two ghosts now, not real characters at all.

Miss McGee's eyes darted about the room but Harriet's were peaceful and calm. 'You're in good hands,' Miss McGee repeated. 'They really know what they're doing. Try not to worry.' She started singing nursery rhymes. '*Little Jack Horner sat in the corner* ... Come on, everyone, I'm sure you all know this one.' Miss McGee's hot thumb on the joints of Harriet's fingers went back and forth, back and forth ... '*I had a little nut tree nothing could it bear but a silver nutmeg and a golden pear* ... '

The doctor nodded away to the tune and so did all the other people in the little white-painted room.

And in the morning, she was woken by a blistering light on her face, for next to her bed was a large picture window, and it must have been a very high floor because when she sat up with the bed-covers clutched to her, and looked out, it seemed as though the whole of London was spread before her: pink and grey, in the unstable haze. A yellow toy train was drawing into St Pancras. The sky was almost blue, the clouds motionless. Opposite a woman was snoring gently, an open novel splayed like a prayer book on her chest.

The pains in Harriet's head and in her stomach were so severe it felt as though the most important parts of her had been stolen, but a doctor appeared, an enormously tall one, and he made a feeble joke to her about lemons and another about starfish (could it have been that?) patting the side of her cheek quite affectionately, a-propos of nothing at all, and, after a short while, a nurse brought her a cup of tea and a plain biscuit, and Harriet thought, not brightly, no, but without a great deal of despair, Look, missus, there have been mornings worse than this that you've survived.

Acknowledgements

'Walk With Me, Oh My Lord', by Estelle White, used by kind permission of McCrimmon Publishing Company Limited.

'London Pride' by Noël Coward copyright © NC Aventales AG 1941, used by permission of Alan Brodie Representation Ltd. www.alanbrodie.com

'I'm Putting All My Eggs In One Basket', Words & Music by Irving Berlin © Copyright 1936 Berlin Irving Music Corporation. Universal Music Publishing Limited for the world excluding United States and Canada. All rights in Sweden, Norway, Denmark, Finland, Iceland & Baltic States administered by Universal/Reuter-Reuter Forlag AB. All Rights Reserved. International Copyright Secured. Used by permission of Music Sales Limited.

'Hi-Lili, Hi-Lo'. Words and Music by Helen Deutsch and Bronislaw Kaper © 1952. Reproduced by permission of EMI Music Publishing, London W8 5SW.

Susie Boyt was born in London and educated at St Catherine's College, Oxford and at University College London. She is the author of four acclaimed novels and a memoir, *My Judy Garland Life*, which was serialised on Radio 4 and will be staged at the Nottingham Playhouse in spring 2013. Since 2002 she has written a weekly column about art and life for the *Financial Times*. She lives in London with her family.